A
Harlequin
Romance

THE LIBRARY TREE

by

LILIAN PEAKE

HARLEQUIN BOOKS TORONTO
WINNIPEG

Original hard cover edition published in 1972
by Mills & Boon Limited, 17 - 19 Foley Street
London W1A 1DR, England

© Lilian Peake 1972

Harlequin edition published October, 1972

SBN 373-01628-X

Printed in Canada

'Madam, a circulating library in a town is as an evergreen tree of diabolical knowledge! It blossoms through the year! And depend on it, Mrs. Malaprop, that they who are so fond of handling the leaves will long for the fruit at last.'

Richard Brinsley Sheridan: *The Rivals*

CHAPTER ONE

THE murmur of voices in the committee room rose and fell like a droning wind in a storm. Carolyn raised the magazine she was pretending to read just a little higher. It helped to shut out the anxiety on the faces of the other girls as they waited, as she was doing, for the verdict of the five men on the other side of that door.

The interviews for the post of library assistant were over. All the applicants could do now was wait for the decision, and it was obvious that they were finding this the hardest part. The other girls were talking and, in their nervousness, giggling a little.

Carolyn wished she could join in, she wished she could throw off this feeling of guilt, of dishonesty, of being a fraud, put down that glossy magazine and walk across to them. She wanted to join in their discussion of the members of that interviewing committee as dispassionately and sometimes as cruelly as they were.

But there was a barrier between them, between herself and those five girls. They did not know it, but she had a foot in the enemy camp. She had, in that room, an uncle who was chairman of the library committee, an alderman, and a powerful influence on the local affairs of this prosperous south coast seaside town. And she knew that he was, at that moment, bringing all his influence to bear on the other members of the committee to get her appointed.

Although her uncle had taken part in the other girls' interviews, he had remained silent during the whole of her own interrogation. This silence had been forced on him by the regulations governing an applicant's relationship to any member of the council.

But she could hear his voice now, overpoweringly

loud as if he couldn't bear any longer the embargo imposed on him by that rule. And it sounded as though he was arguing with someone. There was a voice raised in reply—a hard, bitten-off, angry voice, as if the speaker disagreed violently with what her uncle was saying. Other voices joined in and still the argument went on. The opponent, whoever he was, seemed to be fighting back with insistence, unflagging determination and—in the face of such odds—a sort of desperation, as if the battle had already been lost.

Carolyn wondered, with some amusement, whose voice it was. She could not hear it clearly enough to place it—those committee room doors were almost as thick as the doors of a dungeon—but she felt she would not like to have the owner of that voice as an enemy.

The door was opened and a member of the committee came out.

'Miss Lyle,' he said, and smiled as Carolyn put down the magazine and walked towards him. So her uncle had won.

It was his familiar face she looked for as she entered the room. He was beaming with delight, rocking back in his chair in the manner of a small boy who had just got his own way.

Then someone said, 'We have pleasure in offering you the post of library assistant, Miss Lyle. Are you willing to accept this position?'

She looked at her uncle for reassurance, saw him nodding agitatedly. She moistened her lips, which were strangely parched—she was after all the successful candidate—looked round at the faces watching her expectantly, opened her mouth to reply and caught the expression on the face of the man sitting at the end of the long table. It was so bitter, so angry and so malevolent that she shrank from it. Her lips closed without having made a sound.

'Come along, my dear,' she heard her uncle whisper.

'Give an answer, give an answer.'

She tore her eyes away from that face which had frightened her and came to her senses. 'Yes, thank you,' she murmured in a little-girl voice, as though some one had asked her if she had had a good time at a party.

Four of those five men laughed. They laughed with relief and indulgence—some of them were councillors and had known her for years. The fifth man took up the piece of paper in front of him, crushed it into a tight ball, hurled it into the waste-paper basket and stood up. He was tall, his broad shoulders looked as though they could carry an unlimited amount of responsibility and his eyes, in his strong, darkly handsome face, were blazing with anger. Instinct told her that his had been the voice of the enemy, the bitter adversary of her uncle's persuasiveness.

Carolyn saw her uncle glance at him. He said to her, 'Mr. Hindon's the chief librarian, my dear. He's in charge of the library, so you'll take your orders from him, but there's no need to tell you that, is there?' Austin Bullman stood up. 'Er—Mr. Hindon, my niece, Carolyn. Now a member of your staff.'

The chief librarian looked at her and she felt that his eyes savaged her face. She flushed, not with shyness, but with anger. She grew taut, she stared at him and challenged him back—until she realised that in a few days he would be her boss, and she an insignificant and very junior member of his staff.

Her eyes faltered and lowered to floor level, but when her uncle moved away to speak to one of his friends, she walked along to the man at the other end of the table. Hopefully she searched for some sign in his face which would tell her she had imagined the concentrated hatred that had been implicit in his regard. Perhaps he was not really so bad. Perhaps he had been angry about something else.

She smiled and put out her hand. 'I'm glad I got the

job, Mr. Hindon. I'll—I'll do my best—and work hard.'

He gave a brief nod, gathered up his pens and papers and turned his back on her. Her outstretched hand clenched and fell to her side.

Her uncle took her home. As they drove through the town to the house which Carolyn shared with her grandmother, she wished she could forget the look on the chief librarian's face. She tried to persuade herself that she had imagined his bitter animosity.

She said, willing her uncle to refute her statement and reassure her, 'Mr. Hindon didn't seem very pleased that I was appointed.'

Her uncle laughed and what he said did nothing to still her fears. 'Don't let that worry you. That young man needs taking down a peg or two. He's got to learn that he can't have everything his own way—him and his new ideas. Been pestering the committee ever since he came to make changes. That's all he wants to do—make changes.'

'He hasn't been here long, then?'

'No. Twelve months at the most. He's got to learn who's boss. He thinks *he* is—but I know *I* am. There's a big difference. I'm not the chairman of the library committee for nothing. But I'm not really worried. He's new. He's a new broom. Him and his new ideas,' he said again. 'They won't last, that's one consolation. He'll get so fed up with being stopped in his nonsense, he'll give up fighting, You see, before many more months he'll be as much a member of the Establishment as I am.'

As she listened to her uncle talking, her fears about her immediate future intensified. Now she thought she could see the reason for the chief librarian's attitude. If he and her uncle were such enemies, of course he would not welcome a member of the family on his staff. But she was sure that once he could see that she was willing to work—really work—in her new job, his attitude towards her would change.

'Why didn't he want me to get the job?' she asked. 'Because I'm your niece?'

'Well, there was a lot of that in it, of course. But there were other things. He didn't like the fact that you had a degree. "I don't want a University graduate on my staff," he said. "It's ridiculous having a junior assistant with a degree," he said. "She's twenty-two, much too old," he said. "I'd rather have one of the younger ones, straight out of school, just through their exams. They'd be more willing to learn."' Her uncle laughed and drew up outside Carolyn's house. 'And so on. I just knocked his arguments flying. I had the others with me, too.' He patted her hand 'Don't you worry, my dear. If he tries any funny business, just tell me. I'll soon put Mr. Librarian Hindon in his place. I keep an eye on him as it is, and he doesn't like it. My word, he doesn't like it. But he has to be polite, you know, because I'm the chairman.'

Carolyn rested her hand on the door handle. 'Thanks for that lift, Uncle. And—thanks for everything. Anyway, Gran'll be pleased.'

'She will, my dear. But she won't be surprised. I told her you were going to get the job. I said I wasn't going to let that committee go this afternoon until they'd appointed the right person—and that was you!' She kissed him lightly on the cheek and looked at him.

His figure was plump, his round face cherubic with an aura of geniality about it which was entirely false. Beneath that smile was a nature which was sullenly selfish, relentlessly seeking and as malleable as a chunk of rock. It was a nature that had taken him to the top of his trade and made him into a master builder with an unassailable reputation for quality and value for money. But it was when he tried to apply the tactics which had been so successful in his business life to his dealings with others outside his sphere that his misjudgment brought him up against opposition he could not bear. It was when he came into conflict with a man

11

possessing a determination as strong as his own that trouble started. One of those men was the chief librarian.

But there were times—rare enough—when a softness as melting as a baby's smile showed through and it was with that softness that he now leaned across and kissed his niece.

She responded by saying, 'You're so good to me, Uncle.'

He stretched out his hand and fondled one of the pale gold waist-length plaits which rested against the lapels of her coat. 'You know why, don't you, dear? You're my own flesh and blood. You're my sister's child, and I only do for you what she would have liked to be able to do herself if she'd lived. If I'd had kids of my own—well, you mightn't have been so lucky! But——'

'You've got Donna and Shane.'

'Yes, I know. But they're Maisie's kids, not mine. You're my own flesh and blood,' he repeated.

'And that,' she thought ruefully, 'is just about the most overworked and maddening phrase in Uncle's vocabulary.'

It was, she knew, his one regret—one factor in his life over which he had no control and over which he was irreconcilable—he had not produced an heir, not one child of his own. Her aunt—his first wife Mary—had died childless, reproaching herself for her barren state. His second wife Maisie, a widow, had brought him two children by her first marriage. But even she had never given him the child he longed for—his own flesh and blood.

He accepted now that it was he who was at fault, not Mary, not Maisie, but himself. And as in any situation in which he could not get his own way, it fretted and tormented him.

So Carolyn, his dead sister's child, had taken the place of the daughter he had never had.

Her grandmother was waiting at the front door. She waved to Austin. 'Coming in, son?'

He wound down the car window and thrust his head through. 'Not now, Mother, Too busy.' He waved and was on his way before she could remonstrate with him, She complained to her granddaughter, 'That's all he ever says. Too busy.' She smiled, then asked, as if she already knew the answer, 'Well, dear, how did you get on?'

'I got the job, Gran.'

'I knew you would, dear. Austin told me he'd fix it so you did.'

Carolyn hung up her coat. She said, keeping her face turned away, 'I wish he didn't keep fixing things, Gran.'

'It's his nature, dear, He can't help it. He's not a bit like his sister Beth, your dear mother. He's always been the pushing type. She was always one for keeping in the background.'

'It doesn't sound as though I take after her. Do I, Gran?'

It was a question she had asked many times before. She faced her grandmother and her expression held urgency and sought reassurance. 'Am I like she was?'

Her grandmother went towards the kitchen. 'Yes and no,' she said evasively.

'I'm not shy, Gran,' Carolyn persisted.

'No, you're more like your father,' The distaste in her voice was evident as it always was when Carolyn's father was mentioned. But Carolyn refused to think about her father. She had a mental block where he was concerned. She changed the subject.

'The man called Mr. Hindon—he's the chief librarian, the one in charge—didn't seem very pleased that I was appointed.'

She told her grandmother what had happened, but she shrugged it off. 'Perhaps he didn't see you holding out your hand.'

But Carolyn was convinced he had and the slight he had given her still rankled.

'Are you happy about it? That's what matters. Don't let your uncle push you into anything you don't want.'

'He's done so much for me, Gran, paying for my education, financing me at University——'

'The money's meant nothing to him, dear. He's a rich man now. He's been a good son to me, I'll admit that, the wayl he's supported us both over the years. And Maisie's been good not resenting it. But there's no need for you to feel under any obligation to take the job because of what he's done in the past.'

'It is what I want,' she said slowly, 'but if I'm not welcome, if I've been forced into the job against the wishes of the man in charge....'

'I think you're worrying unnecessarily, Carolyn. You probably won't see a sight of the man from one week to the next. A lot of librarians, your uncle says, don't put their noses outside their offices from one month's end to the other.'

Carolyn wished she could believe her grandmother, but she had the feeling that the man who had turned so pointedly from her outstretched hand was not one of those. He had a force about him, a ruthlessness about his whole bearing which gave her reason to believe that he would know exactly what was going on at any time anywhere in that library.

But, she told herself as she went into the bedroom, she would be much too low down the scale for him to bother about her. She would be a junior assistant, a mere nobody to someone as highly placed as he was. He wouldn't even notice her existence!

She took up her mother's photograph which was standing beside her bed. She gazed at the beautiful face, the quiet eyes, the soft mouth, the short hair curling round the cheeks. She looked at her own reflection in the mirror and raked her features. She sought with near-desperation for some similarity of expres-

14

sion, something in her own face which resembled her mother's, some likeness which would give her that sense of belonging for which she had yearned ever since the day her father had walked away from her for the last time. She could even remember his words.

'Take her,' he had said to her grandmother, 'take the child. I can't look after her any more. I'm not cut out to be a widower, so I'm selling up and getting married again. I can't take the kid with me. Brenda's got three of her own.'

And he had gone without so much as a backward glance. Carolyn had been five years old. She had never seen her father again.

The day she started work at the library was grey and chill, with a scudding March wind. It did nothing at all to enhance the ugly red brick façade of the building, embedded with decades of grime. But, as she climbed the steps to the entrance doors, Carolyn was aware only of a quickening of her pulses and a pleasant sense of anticipation. Those great brown doors were a challenge in themselves and she wanted to get down to work at once and learn everything there was to know about the job.

The doors were closed because the library was not open to the public for another hour. She turned the large black knob, pushed open the door and walked in. She stood there, uncertain and suddenly shy, wishing someone would notice her. There were girls, whom she assumed to be junior assistants, moving along in front of the shelves taking out books and pushing them back into different places. There were others trundling round book-laden trolleys or tidying the tables and pushing in chairs.

Carolyn wondered what to do. She caught the slightly musty smell of the old building and felt a stirring of excitement as her gaze moved round the great room which formed the lending section of the library.

Books, she thought, this is what I've always wanted. Surrounded by books all day, working among them, handling them. . . .

'Can I help you?' A short grey-haired woman was standing at her side, eyeing her with something like distaste, disapproval turning down the corners of her mouth.

'Thank you, yes,' Carolyn told her, grateful to be noticed despite the woman's lack of welcome. 'I'm Carolyn Lyle, the new junior assistant.'

'Yes, I thought you were.' The woman swung away, her plump figure creating a quick cold draught. 'I'll tell the deputy librarian.'

Carolyn followed her to the desk labelled 'Enquiries' and heard her say into an internal telephone, 'Mr. Cotes? Miss Stagg here.' She swung round in her rotating chair and said, with her back to Carolyn, 'Miss Lyle's arrived. Where's she to go?' The woman listened, swivelled round and stared at Carolyn, smiled slightly to herself and turned away again. She lowered her voice and said into the mouthpiece, 'Mr. Hindon said that? I think I see what he means.'

Carolyn flushed. What was that all about? What had Mr. Hindon said? 'All right,' Miss Stagg was saying. 'I'll take her there.' She replaced the receiver and stood up. 'The chief librarian—he's not in yet—has left instructions that you're to work in the stock department. Please follow me.'

She walked across the library, making her way through the shelves stacked with books, to a door marked 'Private' tucked away in a corner. She opened the door, stood back to let Carolyn pass in front of her, called out 'Miss Lyle', as though she were a Master of Ceremonies at an official function, and went out.

Carolyn stood alone again, but this time she was not ignored. The room seemed full of girls, and they had all stopped work to stare with uninhibited curiosity at the newcomer.

16

'Hallo, Miss Lyle,' one of the girls said, breaking away from the group and approaching Carolyn. 'Miss What Lyle?'

Carolyn told her and the girl went on, 'I'm Janet Smithers, this girl with the glasses slipping down her nose is Stella Walker, this is Anne. ...' She stopped. 'I won't tell you any more. You'll have to learn them as you go. There are about a dozen of us. It's a real hen house—battery hens!—and you'd only forget if I told you all their names.'

'Hallo, Carolyn,' said the girl called Stella. 'What have you done to deserve this?' Carolyn looked puzzled and Anne said, 'Welcome to the Outback.'

'What crime have you committed,' Stella persisted, 'that you've been sent to this department?'

'Crime?' Carolyn shook her head, not understanding, so Stella went on, 'Sending a new girl here is like sending someone to Siberia.'

'Don't frighten the poor girl off,' Stella laughed. 'It's her first day.' She told Carolyn, 'Put your things over here. There's a hanger in the cupboard for your coat. Miss Blane will be in in a minute. She's the chief cataloguer. She'll give you a job to do.'

Carolyn removed her coat and searched in her handbag for her compact.

'You engaged?' one of the girls asked. 'No? Just married, then?' Carolyn shook her head. 'Passing time between jobs?' She laughed. 'It's all right. I'm just trying to work out why you've been sent to this department. It's a dead-end job, dear. We come and we go in this section. No one stays here long. It's dead boring at times. You ask Miss Blane when she comes in.'

'No good asking her,' Stella put in. 'She's an expert. She should be—she's specialised in the subject all through her career. Her side of the work *is* interesting. Ours isn't. Routine stuff usually. We'd most of us rather be out there,' she indicated the lending section, 'but His Nibs——'

17

'She means Richard—you know, Mr. Hindon,' Anne interrupted.

'His Nibs didn't consider us intelligent enough, not sufficient up here,' Stella tapped her head, 'so he shoved us in this department.'

The door opened and a tall angular woman in her early fifties came in. Stella introduced Carolyn to her as another poor criminal sent to the condemned cell and Miss Blane smiled and said, 'I'd been told to expect you. Aren't you the one with an uncle who's an alderman?'

Some of the girls gave Carolyn an odd look. Janet saw her embarrassment and said with a laugh, 'Don't hold it against her, though. You can't visit the sins of the uncles on the nieces——' She clapped her hand over her mouth. 'What am I saying?'

Carolyn laughed, 'It's all right. When you've got a relative who's a public figure, you have to accept the criticisms along with the praise—if any. I've got used to it.'

'What's his name, Carolyn?' one of the girls asked. 'Lyle?'

'No, Bullman,' Carolyn said.

There was a heavy unbelieving silence. 'Did you say Bullman, chairman of the library committee?'

'Afraid so.'

Janet drew in her breath. 'No wonder you've been sent to Siberia! Express orders of the librarian himself, no doubt.' The others tried to silence her, but she rushed on. 'He hates your uncle's guts. You've only got to mention the word Bullman in his presence and he becomes like a raging bull himself.'

Miss Blane said sharply, 'That's enough, Janet. You have some work to do, I presume?'

Janet took the hint and walked away.

'Now, Miss Lyle,' Miss Blane smiled reassuringly, 'the first thing you've got to do is to put out of your mind what the girls have told you about this department.

The library just wouldn't work without us.' She ignored the ironic tittering of the others and looked round the room. 'You might even compare it with the engine room of a ship. This department is as important as that. We control the intake of all the new books that come in, and we prepare them for issue to the public not only through this library, which as you know is the central one—but all the branch libraries in the area.'

She stood at her desk. 'When my senior assistant comes in, I'll hand you over to her.' The door opened and a tall serious-looking girl in her late twenties appeared. 'Ah, here she is.'

Miss Blane introduced her as Pearl Matthews.

'Let's start at the beginning,' Pearl said. 'First we unpack the parcels—that's something you'll be doing——'

'*Ad nauseam*,' someone broke in.

Pearl smiled and went on, 'Then the books are marked off against the invoices and we make sure there are none missing. Then the name of the library they're intended for is stamped on them. After that there's a process called accessioning—this gives every book a number, and so on. You'll learn it all as you go along. If I tell you everything now, you'll only forget.'

Pearl led Carolyn to the other side of the room. 'The only way to tackle this unpacking job,' Pearl told her, indicating the parcels which covered the floor, 'is to get down to it. One of the girls will give you some scissors, and tell you where to find the invoices and how to check them through.' She smiled at Carolyn. 'Ever been behind the scenes in a library before? You'll find it something of a shock.'

Anne looked up, 'I bet you didn't expect all this donkey work. Dead boring, this is.'

'Come on, Carolyn,' Stella urged, 'here are the scissors.' She lifted a parcel of books and put them on the floor at Carolyn's feet. 'Get snipping on those, will you?'

Carolyn crouched down and cut the string. 'Is this all you do?' she asked. 'This routine stuff?'

She was frowning and for the first time doubt stirred in her mind. She was not reassured by Stella's next words. 'Routine's our second name, dear.'

Mechanically, Carolyn snipped at string, peeled off brown paper, searched for invoices and checked them against the contents of each parcel. She was puzzled. She remembered Miss Stagg's words—'the chief librarian has left instructions'—so it was a directive from him. If what the girls were saying was true, was it his way of keeping her shut away, out of sight and out of mind?

There was a break for coffee and then they got down to work again. It was nearly lunch-time when a man came into the room, a man of medium height with greying hair and kindly eyes. He talked to Miss Blane, who looked in Carloyn's direction and nodded her head.

The man walked across the room. 'Miss Lyle?' Carolyn rose and stood unsteadily, her back stiff from bending. 'I'm Graham Cotes, deputy librarian. How do you do?' He held out his hand. 'You remember me? I was on the interviewing committee.'

Of course I remember you, Carolyn thought. You were the nicest person there. 'How are you getting on?' he asked.

She knew the others were listening. 'Quite—quite well, thank you,' she replied, because there was nothing else she could say.

'What you expected?'

'Well, it—it's . . .' She managed to compromise. 'Yes and no.'

He laughed and consulted his watch. 'I'd like a word with you.' He looked at Miss Blane. 'Can you spare her?'

She murmured 'Of course' and Mr. Cotes led the

way to the door. They climbed the steep wide staircase, the stone treads glistening as the light caught them through the high arched windows. The corridor was dark. Here and there the paint was peeling off the yellowed walls and the place had a sombre, uncared-for air about it.

'I must tell my uncle.' The thought was there in her mind, and she was barely conscious of it.

Mr. Cotes showed her into his office, a small, un-carpeted room with little comfort. He sat at his desk and invited Carolyn to take the chair opposite him.

He smiled and seemed to be trying to put her at her ease. 'It's not often,' he said, 'that we have an alderman's niece come to work here,'

On her guard at once, Carolyn tried to scent out the slightest hint of sarcasm, but none was there. If her glance had not told her that he was honest and sincere, his voice and his smile would have done. It was obvious that he did not share his superior's rejection of Alderman Bullman's niece.

'Are you,' she asked, knowing that she need not be afraid of this man, 'trying to give me the red carpet treatment? Because there's no need. I've come to work.'

He laughed with some relief. 'Well, to be honest, I was wondering how to treat you. Now I know. As one of us.'

And that, Carolyn thought, is almost the nicest thing anyone could say to me. He seemed to recognise her pleasure. 'But you've a long way to go, you know, before you can consider yourself fully qualified. There are exams to pass, important ones. But you'll take them in your stride.'

She looked at him. He was so approachable, this man, that she decided she could speak to him frankly. 'Mr. Cotes,' she said, hesitated, then went on, 'will I—will I always stay there, in that department?'

He stiffened a little. 'Why, what's wrong with it?'

'Nothing—nothing really, except—well, from what

the girls tell me——' she stopped, finding it more difficult than she thought to put her doubts into words, 'they say they're only short-term staff, that most of the girls who work there soon leave. They—they call it "being sent to Siberia." '

She stopped, aghast at having given the others away. But Mr. Cotes was laughing. 'So that's what they call it! Take no notice, Miss Lyle, it's just girlish chatter. It's a vital department. But thank you for telling me something I didn't know—that is, how isolated they appear to feel from the rest of us. I'll have to try to remedy that. I suppose,' he went on, 'you thought, like a lot of other people, that librarianship consisted exclusively of standing at the counter stamping books and issuing tickets?'

Carolyn laughed and nodded, ashamed of her admission. She asked, brightening a little, 'How does one become a cataloguer, Mr. Cotes?'

'A cataloguer?' He laughed. 'It's early days to be thinking in those specialised terms. Cataloguing is not something that can be tackled by a newcomer. But after attending library school—that's something you will probably be doing after about a year, once you've made up your mind that you would like to make librarianship your career—you'll have qualified and then you would be able to tackle cataloguing.' He brushed back his hair and Carolyn noticed how grey it was.

'But we've all had to start at the bottom, you know, at floor level, as it were, if not by unpacking parcels then by doing other kinds of routine duties—even chief librarians and their deputies have had to.' He added with a twinkle, 'Even Mr. Hindon.'

He was leaning back in his chair, quite at ease, and the tension which had been gnawing at Carolyn all day began to lose its bite. She grew happier, more hopeful and less worried about her position.

The door was thrust open and a man walked in.

'Talk of the devil,' said Graham Cotes easily.

The room temperature seemed to take a dive as Richard Hindon fixed his gaze on the girl sitting relaxed in the chair. He watched her stiffen, rise and look at him, her glance wavering as she waited for him to speak. She felt ridiculously guilty as though she had committed an unforgivable crime.

Mr. Cotes rose and moved his hand in an introductory gesture. 'You two met, I believe, at the interview?'

Richard Hindon's nod was brief and rude. 'Intentionally so,' Carolyn thought, anger rising in her like mercury in a thermometer.

'Would you credit it, Richard,' Mr Cotes sat down again, 'she's talking already about learning cataloguing. Been here a few hours and she wants to plunge in at the deep end!'

The chief librarian did not share his deputy's good humour. 'I trust,' he said without the flicker of a smile 'you told Miss Lyle the qualities that are essential for such work—accuracy, patience and method. Not to mention that elusive thing called intelligence.'

'I'm sure she's got all those things. Haven't you, Miss Lyle?'

Carolyn did not reply.

'Well, Miss Lyle?' She looked up at the sharp tone of the man in charge.

'Whatever I say, Mr. Hindon,' she answered quietly, 'will put me in the wrong. If I say "yes", you could accuse me of being big-headed. If I say "no", then you would no doubt dismiss me as a nonentity.'

'I'll tell you the best way out of it, Miss Lyle,' Mr. Cotes intervened, enjoying the joke. 'Say "time will tell," It's a nice vague, non-committal answer.' He looked at the other man. 'She's worried, Richard, because she thinks she's been condemned to the equivalent of life imprisonment. She's convinced she's been sent to "Siberia". And all because you directed her to the stock department. I'm sure she thinks you did it to

23

get her out of the way.' His laugh dismissed the idea.

'She could be right.' The words hit her like a shower of glass and were just as dangerous. Mr. Cotes frowned, uncertain at last.

'I'm going out,' the chief librarian said, and Carolyn was ignored as the two men talked. So now she knew the truth. She was to be treated by this man as a criminal, committed to hard labour—unpacking parcels—until she got so sick and tired of it that she left. That was his way of saying "Get out, fast."

She licked her lips and looked at Mr. Cotes. 'Shall I go?'

Mr. Cotes was on his feet at once. 'I'm so sorry, Miss Lyle.' His politeness was in sharp contrast with the other man's calculated bad manners. 'We'll continue our chat another time. If there's ever anything worrying you, come straight to me, won't you, and I'll do my best to sort things out.'

She smiled at him warmly, frowned uncertainly at the chief librarian, who was standing tall and rigid, hands thrust into his pockets, near the door.

'Miss Lyle,' he said curtly as she was about to leave, 'come and see me this afternoon at five o'clock.'

'Yes, Mr. Hindon.' She walked away, her heart beating heavily, her anxieties revived.

She rejoined the girls and Anne said, 'You're getting V.I.P. treatment, aren't you? A mere junior getting a welcome from the deputy?' She laughed, but Carolyn was sure she could detect a note of jealousy.

She said, 'You couldn't be more wrong, Anne.' But she didn't elaborate, nor did she tell her about the summons to the chief's office later that afternoon.

At lunch-time, as they sat eating their sandwiches in a corner of the stock room—there was nowhere else for them to go—Pearl Matthews said, 'Forgive me for saying so, Carolyn, but you seem to be a little—well, old to be starting on the junior grade.'

'You're quite right, Pearl, but you see, I started

24

training to be a teacher, then decided I wasn't made of the right stuff.' She said nothing about her years at University or about her degree. Somehow she felt that it would make the others regard her as 'different', as an oddity even. 'I've enough against me,' she thought, 'without adding to my troubles.'

Carolyn looked at her watch and saw with a jerk of fear that it was five o'clock. Her shoes gritted on the stone staircase and she hovered, uncertain and nervous, outside the door marked, in large letters, 'Chief Librarian.' The door next to it was opened and a young woman eyed her questioningly. 'Can I help you?'

The voice was deep and purring, the smile slow, the eyes thoughtful as they moved over Carolyn's flushed face, and down, down to the ends of the long golden plaits. 'You're Miss Lyle?' the voice asked affectedly. 'Of course you are. I recognise you by Mr. Hindon's description.'

Carolyn would not even let herself wonder about the words the chief librarian had probably used to describe her.

'He's engaged,' she said, retreating into her office and inviting Carolyn to follow. 'Mr. Cotes is with him. He shouldn't be long.' She found a magazine and put it into Carolyn's hands. 'Sit down. Make yourself comfortable. My name's Harvey, by the way, Roseanna Harvey.' She went to the door. 'I'm going home.'

She paused, and looked Carolyn up and down. Her interest was frank and her expression held a tincture of distaste as she said, 'So you're the famous—or should I say infamous—Miss Lyle. Alderman Bullman's secret weapon.' She put her hand to her mouth with mock anxiety. 'Oh, don't tell him I said that, will you? I'd better mind what I say from now on.'

So the chief librarian had injected his toxin into his secretary. How long would it be, Carolyn wondered

25

helplessly as the door closed, leaving her alone, before the entire staff was poisoned against her?

She turned the pages of the magazine, and her eyes scanned the words without taking in their meaning. She heard the two men talking in the adjoining room. She tried to shut her ears to what they were saying. Desperately she concentrated on the illustrations in front of her, read the captions, studied the recipes, but the voices were raised to such a pitch that she had to overhear.

'Now I'm landed with his damned niece,' Richard Hindon was saying, 'and there's no need for you to lay it on so thick, Graham.' There was an interruption, but it did not last. 'You can't deny it, I saw you chatting her up this morning. For God's sake don't soft-soap her, we'll never get rid of her.' The voice ground on. 'What's the good of a degree in a public library? With her background, she won't know what work is. Timid creature from the look of her, weak-kneed, browbeaten by the uncle. Useless type. . . . I don't want her here. She'll probably act as a spy for the old devil. He makes my life difficult enough, and now I've got a relative of his wished on me, I won't be able to keep him away from the place. I'll just have to make her life hell, so that she leaves.'

The other voice, softer, more kindly, said urgently, 'Couldn't you try being nice to her and get some of these things you want that way? She might be able to persuade the uncle to act more favourably towards you.'

There was an explosion from the other man. 'Be *nice* to her? Do you mean *use* her? Are you asking me to be a hypocrite?' He seemed to make a vicious noise with his throat. 'When I get going on her, she'll run away so fast you won't see her for the cloud of dust kicked up by her shapely legs.'

Carolyn pressed her hands to her throat, then moved them to her ears. She had to shut out that voice, those words which were grinding her self-confidence and her self-respect to dust.

The door handle moved. Someone was coming in. She had to compose herself. She grasped her handbag and stood up. Graham Cotes smiled when he saw her, but his eyes were guarded.

'Hallo, Miss Lyle. Been here long?'

'Not very,' she lied, and he seemed relieved.

'Richard,' he called, 'your new member of staff is here to see you.' He patted her shoulder as he passed and whispered, 'Good luck.' He had gone before she could thank him.

CHAPTER TWO

CAROLYN had never seen eyes so cold or so critical as Richard Hindon's as she faced him across his desk. They were eyes which made her want to switch on a heater to warm her shivering, shaking thoughts. Curtly he told her to sit down. He remained standing.

She looked up at him and noticed that his dark hair sprang thickly back from his forehead. There was a trapped energy about him which he seemed to have difficulty in controlling. His fingers were a restless, searching extension of his mind and they were moving now over the articles which covered his desk. They came to rest on the back of his chair.

He broke the silence at last. 'I've called you in here,' he said, 'not because of your semi-privileged status—being the niece of your aldermanic uncle—but because I want to inform you quite frankly of what is involved in this job you've taken on.' He sat down. 'I'm telling you in order to give you the opportunity of leaving now and giving some other girl a chance—a girl without your moderate academic achievement but with a great deal more potential to offer than you appear to have. Now,' he sat back as though preparing for a long siege, 'you have a degree. You can forget that.'

He opened a drawer and pulled out a sheet of paper. 'I see from your application form that you didn't finish your year of teacher-training following on the completion of your degree.' He threw the form on to his desk. 'I have no doubt that you won't stick at this job either, because one of the most important qualities a would-be librarian must have is staying power. It would appear from your record that you just haven't got it.'

She wanted to deny his charges, but he gave her no

chance to interrupt. 'I've been lumbered with you by your uncle, but I need not worry. It won't be long before you walk out of the door and make a graceful and final exit from the building.'

She said, still hoping to make contact with the reasonable side of his nature, 'I should like to explain, Mr. Hindon, that I left teacher-training half-way through because I realised I didn't possess the right qualities to make a teacher. I also knew I wouldn't like it as a career.'

'So you think you will "like" librarianship better?' He gave the word an insulting emphasis.

'Well,' she answered, a hint of uncertainty slowing her speech, 'I've always liked books so——'

'You think a *liking for books* is the sole criterion by which you judge an aptitude for a library career?'

His sarcasm, his deliberate belittling of her intelligence, made her despair. 'I imagine it goes a long way towards it and——' he tried to interrupt, but she went on, 'as a child I never possessed many books of my own although I always wanted them. We—we couldn't afford them....'

'So you're coming to work here,' he cut in, 'for psychological reasons, to compensate for a lack of books in childhood, to fulfil a lifelong need?' His incredulous smile unnerved her as much as the contempt implicit in his words.

'I feel it necessary to emphasise, Miss Lyle, that far more than a liking for books is required to make a successful librarian. It isn't a job where you keep your hands clean and can quietly go to sleep. It requires stamina, dedication, a willingness to learn and to take orders. Intelligence is vital, so is accuracy, orderliness and—I must repeat this—persistence. The hours are long, the work demanding.' He smiled condescendingly. 'Now if, after all that, you wish to pick up your handbag and go—well, don't mind me, do just that. No doubt your uncle will find you another post as he

29

did this one—by using his influence.'

She said quietly, meeting the challenge in his eyes, 'I'm not leaving, Mr. Hindon, not even if you force me to scrub the floors—which no doubt you would if you legally could.'

There was a prolonged silence. He flicked through the pages of a book lying on his desk, then he transferred his gaze to her face. He looked at her thoughtfully, and said, 'You know, this liaison, this twisted sort of connection between myself and your uncle with you acting as intermediary, might prove—how shall I put it—tactically remunerative.'

'Do you mean,' she asked, 'that you have set aside your principles and have decided to "use" me?'

'"Use" you?' he rapped out, momentarily disconcerted. 'What are you talking about?'

She lowered her eyes and stroked the soft leather of her handbag. 'I—I heard what you were saying while I was waiting in your secretary's room.'

'Did you now?' He raised his eyebrows. 'What I said was not intended for your ears.' He considered his words carefully. 'Yes, it could cut both ways. If I tread carefully enough, I could "get" at your uncle through you, just as he no doubt will be "getting at" me, also through you.'

She asked angrily, 'What will you do, Mr. Hindon, hold me to ransom, say you'll make my life a misery unless I call my uncle off? Or perhaps use my "good offices", my persuasive tactics as a favourite niece to make him change his mind about something, some decision he might be forcing on you?'

He looked at her narrowly and she flushed. 'Don't put ideas into my head, Miss Lyle. It could be dangerous.' Still he watched her face. 'One thing I've discovered about you. I made a gross misjudgment of your personality. You're not the timid, shrinking creature I imagined you were on first acquaintance.'

'I suppose,' she cried, 'you think that's a pity. I

suppose it means you've realised you can't bully me out of the job as you thought you could, because I'm not a shy, unsophisticated school-leaver.' He didn't answer, merely moved his eyebrows expressively and she began to hate him.

She hated him for his contempt, for his arrogance, for the ice in his eyes. She hated the way he made her feel an interloper, a usurper of another's place, an insignificant, mindless adolescent. She could not forgive him for his air of self-sufficiency, for his obvious lack of the need for close contact with any other human being.

She had never felt such hatred before and it ate into her thoughts as nothing else had ever done in the whole of her life.

His smile, which touched only his mouth, was deliberately goading. 'I suppose you'll go home now and give your uncle a verbatim account of all that has taken place between us.'

'It's not a habit of mine to tell tales.'

'No? Well, time will tell. Anything you carry to him will come back to me. It's inevitable. The grapevine in local government is pretty efficient.'

He watched her sitting rigid before him. 'I can see you're outraged at what I've been saying to you.' She began to reply, but he raised his hand and silenced her. 'Don't deny it. It's all over your face.' He leaned back in his seat, one arm draped negligently over the back of the chair, his attitude careless and indifferent, showing with every inch of his body that he was in complete command of the situation. 'Let me assure you that I don't usually greet new members of staff in this way. I might add that neither do I call juniors into my office to bid them welcome. I made an exception of you, though—for obvious reasons.'

His arrogance robbed her of speech and the silence grew so long, she began to fidget. Her colour rose and she flicked a long golden plait of hair round to her back, an unconscious gesture in moments of stress.

She said, making a final attempt to reach the humanity he must surely possess, 'Mr. Hindon, when I knew I'd got this job. I was very pleased. It was something I had longed to do for years, and I started work here determined to make a success of it. But it seems that where you're concerned, just because I'm—who I am, that simply isn't enough.' She fought to keep her voice steady and it rose against her will on a note of appeal. 'Given the chance, I'm sure I would be able to prove even to you that I could succeed in librarianship, that I've got the necessary intelligence and ability to do so.' She stood up, but he motioned her to sit down again. By the coldness of his eyes she knew that she had not come even within touching distance of his compassion.

'Miss Lyle,' he said softly, moving his blotter into the exact centre of his desk top, then flicking his eyes up to meet hers, 'I have one more thing to say. I hold the trump card.'

She stared at him, the question in her eyes turning into fear as she saw a twisted kind of anticipation in his smile. He said, 'Not only are you here on six months' probation—I could bring about your dismissal if I wished at any time within that period—but I could void your appointment here and now.' His eyes did not leave hers. 'On the day of your interview, your uncle broke the rules. You may remember that on your application form you had to declare any relationship to any member of the council——' Carolyn nodded and he went on, 'so as a relative of yours, he should not have come within a mile of that committee room, let alone sat on the committee itself.'

'But,' she whispered, 'he took no part in my actual interview.'

'Maybe not, but he took part—quite volubly—in the discussion which followed the interviews. He presented your case in overpoweringly convincing terms, and, as you now know, the members of that committee, with one exception,' again that unpleasant smile, 'were convinced. So I have only to pick up that telephone,' he stretched out his hand and rested it tantalisingly on the receiver, 'dial the number of a certain Alderman Battry—who, to put it mildly, hates your uncle's guts —tell him the truth and thus, by devious methods, make your appointment null and void. Just like that.' He clicked his fingers in the air.

He sat back, folded his arms and waited for her to react. With something like satisfaction, he watched her bewilderment, her dismay and her unbelieving tears. Then he pulled a pile of papers towards him and with an abrupt movement of the hand dismissed her.

As she walked slowly away along the corridor, her eyes picked out the paint peeling from the walls. The thought which had stolen into her mind that morning crept back—'I must tell my uncle'. Now she knew that, come what may, where that library was concerned, she must never 'tell her uncle' anything.

Pretending to her grandmother that she had enjoyed her first day at work was the hardest thing Carolyn had ever had to do. As she looked into her grandmother's searching eyes, saw the anxious love in her lined face, she knew that she must never let her even begin to guess that anything was wrong.

It was harder still to parry her uncle's probing questions when she telephoned him that evening as he had asked her to do.

'Well,' he asked, with teasing affection, 'enjoyed yourself? Glad I pulled those strings and got you in? Did you get all the tickets mixed up and give everyone the wrong books?'

'I—I haven't been in the lending section, Uncle.' She tried desperately to keep her tone light. 'I'm a backroom girl.'

'How d'you mean?' His voice was sharp.

'I've been in a—a much more important place—the

stock department, where things like cataloguing are done. You know, behind the scenes,' she forced a laugh, 'where they do all the real work.'

'Oh, I see now. They've been teaching you all about the cataloguing business, have they? Very important that, very important. Hindon's got more sense than I credited him with. Expect he realises how good you are now he's seen you at close quarters.'

She felt hysteria rising, she wanted to shriek with mirthless laughter at the irony of it all. What would he say, she thought, if I told him his wonderful niece, with her University degree, had been kneeling on the floor all day unpacking endless parcels?

'I'll call in in a day or two,' he promised, 'just to see how you're getting on.'

'No, no, Uncle,' she rushed in, 'don't do that. Give me—give me a chance to settle down a bit. It might put me off if you came in!'

He laughed heartily. 'Shy then, are you? Of your old uncle? All right, lass, I'll keep away for a bit.' She heard him speak to someone. 'Don't go away, lass, here's Shane. His tongue's hanging out to speak to you.' She heard a loud stage whisper at the other end, 'Taking her out tonight, lad, to celebrate her first day at work?'

The receiver must have changed hands because she heard in her ear, 'Well, sweetie, am I?'

'What, taking me out?' The idea had a sudden appeal. If her step-cousin, with his smooth tongue, his brash self-assurance and his open admiration, could not wash away the nasty taste left behind by her disastrous interview with the chief librarian, then no one could. She knew that he was the only one in the family to whom she could tell the truth, and the need to unburden herself to someone discreet and sympathetic was becoming urgent. 'Why not?'

'Right. Dress up, darling.' He named a large hotel on the sea front.

'But that's expensive, Shane.'

'Maybe it is, but money means nothing to me, you know that. It overflows from my pockets on to the floor.' He laughed. 'I'm rolling in it.'

He could be right, Carolyn thought. He was, after all, a partner, if only a junior one, in a thriving firm of estate agents in the town. His stepfather had financed him, persuaded him to qualify—he just scraped through his exams—and then used his influence to push him into the largest estate agents he could find. It was common knowledge that the carrot he had offered the owner of the firm was the sole agency for the sale of his own houses. And there was a constant and unceasing local demand for Bullman-built properties.

'Anyway,' Shane said, 'now you're a working girl, you can pay your share, can't you?'

She laughed. 'In that case, you'll have to wait until the end of the month. I don't get paid till then.'

'All right, I'll accept an IOU at the end of the evening.' He lowered his voice. 'Unless you'd care to pay me in other ways?'

'That, my dear Shane,' she thought, 'is something I'll never do. And you know it.' She liked him, he was fun and it pleased her uncle to see them together. But as far as she was concerned, there never could be anything more between them.

'You know the answer to that, Shane,' she said aloud. 'What time will you call?'

He'd give her half an hour, he said, and rang off.

By the time Shane's car drew up outside, the memory of that interview had ebbed away. She knew the tide would come in again later, in the darkness of the night, but she would enjoy the next few hours as though nothing had happened.

Shane whistled when he saw her, as she knew he would. He did the same to any girl, whether she was beautiful or just moderately attractive. But she was aware that she was looking her best. And she was in a reckless, rather desperate mood. There was nothing right with her world, but she was determined to do her damnedest to pretend there was nothing wrong.

The hotel dining-room was low-timbered, and softly flickering scarlet candles cast moving shadows around the walls. There were flowers in pottery vases and tall green-stemmed glasses beside each place-setting. Soft sweet music enhanced the intimate atmosphere and Carolyn sighed with pleasure as she settled into her seat.

She returned Shane's smile, noting how his attractive features were becoming spoilt by too much self-indulgence in drink and food. But his good nature made her forgive him for a lot of things and when he put his hand over hers as it rested on the table, she tolerated his touch and did not reject it as she usually did. He raised her hand and put it to his lips with an unusually gallant gesture.

When she looked surprised he said, 'It's obvious you're in a bad mood, so I'm wooing you into a good one.'

So much for my 'disguise', she thought. As an actress I'm a total failure, She frowned and let her gaze wander, trying to think of a witty reply.

She caught her breath. It was as improbable as snow in midsummer, but it was true. He was there, sitting alone at a corner table across the narrow room, the man she had grown to hate with all her being. Richard Hindon was dining at the same hotel and their eyes met, sparked and burst into flame like fireworks out of control.

Following on the surprise, there was cynicism in the look he flicked from her to Shane and back again, and there was rejection and contempt besides. She tightened with anger that this should have happened, that he should have invaded her moments of pleasure and shattered her hard-won peace of mind with a single salvo from his eyes.

Shane watched her expression change and followed her gaze. 'Who's that handsome blighter? Know him, sweetie? He's looking as though he knows you. Is he one of your guilty secrets? Part of your past or,' he took her hand again with a possessive gesture, 'part of your present?'

She shook her head vigorously, and said, her lips trembling a little, 'If I could tell you, Shane——'

'Tell me, darling, unburden yourself——' He stopped as the waiter approached and they consulted the menu together. Shane ordered, took out a cigarette, drew it to life with the flame of a candle and said, 'Right. I'm all ears.'

She told him in detail about her interview with the chief librarian that afternoon, and as she spoke, she lived through it all again. When she had finished talking she ventured a glance at the man in the corner and found to her chagrin that he was still watching her. She told Shane, and slowly, deliberately, he half-turned in his seat to stare openly at the man they had been discussing. But he had already moved his eyes to the food which the waiter was putting before him.

Shane tapped on the table with his finger-tips. 'It's difficult, Carolyn, and I doubt if there's much you can do about it at present. You'll just have to stick it for a few months, then tell Dad you've decided you don't like the work.'

'But, Shane, I've changed my mind once before in the middle of my training, when I decided I didn't want to be a teacher. How can I back out of this job as well?'

'Well, darling, there's one thing you can't tell Dad and that's the truth. He moved heaven and earth to get you in there, even broke the rules, as he says over there.' He moved his head in Richard Hindon's direction.

The waiter brought their food and left them. Shane

went on, 'You know, arrogant as that so-and-so in the corner may be, I think I can see his point of view. Judging by what Dad's said, he pesters the life out of him. Every decision the poor chap makes, Dad insists on the right to refer it back to the committee first, even when the subject in question comes under the librarian's jurisdiction.'

'But, Shane,' her eyes became appealing, 'why take it out on me? I've done him no harm.'

'No, duckie,' he patted her hand, 'but he's obviously taking no chances. It's just hard luck on you.' They ate in silence for a while, then Shane said, 'I remember when Hindon was appointed, Dad wondered whether they'd done right. He was too young for the job, Dad said. What could he know about a top job like that when he was only thirty-six? It turned out he knew a lot. But, according to Dad, he had all the wrong ideas, and was quite ruthless in trying to shove them through the committee.'

'Ruthless should be his second name,' Carolyn muttered, looking across at the man she was talking about. 'You should have heard the way he talked to me.' Then, as if he felt her eyes upon him, he moved his eyes towards her and narrowed them unpleasantly.

Confused, she grabbed her glass of wine and with it managed somehow to hide the flush which crept over her cheeks. What does he think I'm doing, she wondered bitterly, spying on his private life?

'Carolyn,' Shane's voice called her attention back to him. He lifted a plait of her hair, fondled it and put it to his lips. Embarrassed beyond words, because she knew Richard Hindon was looking, she snapped, 'Don't, Shane.'

'Why not?' he whispered, 'scared your boss might disapprove? You never know, it might give him ideas, make him want to humour a beautiful woman instead of abusing her.' He studied her face. 'And when you're angry, with that colouring and those blue eyes, you're

38

breathtaking. You'd make any normal male want to take you in his arms and kiss your anger away.'

She flushed at his blatant flattery, realised he was trying to help her and began to adjust to his mood. When he leaned across and put his lips to her cheek, she didn't resist. When he took her hand and stroked it, she didn't stop him. When he whispered jokes in her ear, her laughter was out of all proportion to their worth. The more disgusted the man in the corner became, the more she acted the abandoned sophisticate.

'Coffee is served in the lounge, sir, madam.' The waiter bowed them out of the room.

Away from Richard Hindon's presence, Carolyn's gay mood petered out. Shane led her to an armchair and left her, saying he had spotted some important clients at the other end of the room.

'Don't be long, will you, Shane?' she urged.

'Why, darling, afraid the dragon will come in and devour you to round off his meal?'

She smiled weakly and was alone until the waiter carried in the coffee. Shane was still deep in conversation, so she poured a cup for herself. She was in the act of raising the cup to her lips when Richard Hindon filled the doorway, gazed round, spotted her and wandered towards her. Hastily she returned her cup to the saucer, prepared for flight, feeling like the cornered victim of a murderer about to pounce.

He seemed to be hesitating about which chair to choose and she could not keep the fear from her eyes. She followed his every movement and watched his protracted indecision. By the open amusement on his face, she knew he was aware of her fear, which by now was amounting to an irrational terror.

He hesitated so long about his choice of chair that she became convinced he was doing it to torment her. He looked across at the one next to hers, eyed the couch, moved towards it and changed his mind. With his hands slipped into his pockets he turned and studied the prints of ancient steam locomotives which were placed at regular intervals round the walls. She knew there was one above her head. She sat there, her muscles tight, her body perspiring, waiting for him to get round to it.

Frantically she looked for Shane, tried to signal to him that the coffee was there, but he did not see her signs. She looked again at Richard Hindon and as she did so his eyes moved away from her back to the pictures on the walls. Slowly, deliberately, he made his way round the room, not stopping even when the waiter put his tray of coffee on the table, until he reached the print above her head.

He muttered an exaggeratedly polite 'If you will excuse me,' and stood directly in front of her, his legs brushing her knees, staring at the picture on the wall. She wanted to scream, she wanted to use her hands, her feet, to push him away, she felt that a mad animal inside her was clamouring to be released.

She stared up at him, breathing hard, her teeth clenched inside her lips, the fury that she was feeling concentrated in her eyes. He glanced down and, judging by the satisfaction on his face, he must have seen the effect he was having on her. He smiled coolly, lazily and insultingly and walked away.

The cause of her tension gone, Carolyn slumped back. She felt as though she had come through a terrible ordeal and she was aghast at herself for submitting to the power he seemed to have over her. Sulky now, she watched him bend forward and pour out his coffee. He raised his cup, leaned back in the armchair and crossed his legs. She turned and at last caught Shane's eye.

He signalled to her that he was coming, said goodbye to his acquaintance and made his way across the room. He threw himself on to the couch, patted the cushion next to him and she moved at his invitation. He took his coffee from her, she picked up her own and with Shane's arm round her waist, they drank.

Then they talked, and all the while Carolyn was conscious of being watched. Although Richard Hindon was resting his head against the back of the armchair, although his eyes appeared to be closed, she knew that he was keeping them under constant surveillance.

Shane whispered, 'The dragon is somnolent after his feed.'

Carolyn laughed. She began to act again. She moved closer to Shane, rested her head on his shoulder and smiled up at him as though he was the only man in the world she cared for. Shane responded as she knew he would, by murmuring endearments, kissing her cheek and gazing into her eyes.

A woman appeared in the doorway. She was attractive, brown-haired and well-dressed. She looked round, spotted Richard Hindon and made for him. He rose slowly and scowled at her.

'Hallo, Richard,' they heard her say, 'I've settled the kids down and thought I'd drop in for a drink.' She beckoned to the waiter and when he approached them her companion took over. He ordered, sat back and waited for her to start talking. She did, non-stop, and his face took on an acutely bored expression.

Carolyn whispered, 'If that's his wife, then I pity her. Look how he's treating her.'

Shane said softly, 'I rather hope she's not his wife, sweetie. I could go for her, given half a chance. All that shapeliness! My word, some men don't know when they're lucky.'

'Sorry to disappoint you, Shane,' Carolyn murmured, 'but she must be his wife. Can't you see her rings?'

'You're right.' He turned down the corners of his mouth. 'There goes my dream girl.'

Carolyn laughed, 'Every pretty girl you see is your dream girl.'

The newcomer turned her head at their laughter and stared at them. She whispered something to her companion, who nodded his head irritably and whispered back. The woman turned again and stared, this time with even greater interest, first at Carolyn, whom she inspected thoroughly, then, smiling, she moved her gaze to Shane. Her inspection of him was even more thorough and her smile a little warmer.

'You've made a conquest, Shane,' Carolyn murmured, looking down at her hands.

'Whoever heard of a wife with a roving eye?' Shane tittered into her ear. 'And in full view of her husband, too. He obviously doesn't spank her enough.'

Carolyn was silent. As Shane casually used the word 'husband', she became aware of a tension somewhere inside her which, try as she might, she could not throw off. So he was married, that unpleasant, ill-mannered, overbearing man. He had a wife and family. In spite of herself, her heart went out to the woman who was sitting with him, doing her best to talk him out of his ill humour.

Carolyn stirred restlessly, looked at her watch and suggested that it was time to go. Shane agreed and as they rose Richard Hindon's wife turned her head quickly, smiled at them both and said, brightly, 'Goodnight.'

Shane raised his hand and replied with a smile that equalled hers in warmth. The man sitting beside her scowled and looked away.

When Carolyn opened the stock-department door the following morning, Anne greeted her with a pair of scissors, pushed a parcel of books towards her and said, 'Get snipping on those, Carolyn, fast. Rumour has it the chief's on the prowl.'

'He's having one of his periodic inspections,' Stella said. 'He usually does it without warning, but this time the grapevine's been extra efficient.'

'Don't let him catch you slacking, Carolyn,' Anne put in. 'Not even your semi-V.I.P. status would be enough to save you, if he did.'

Miss Blane called the girls to order and there was silence for a while. Every time the door opened the girls would turn, expecting to see the man in charge come in. Carolyn did not turn her head with the others. If Richard Hindon did appear, she would rather become part of the furniture, merge into the tables and shelves, than be singled out by his sardonic eyes for special attention.

When he did not come, tension slackened and the chatter rose to its usual level. As Carolyn cut string, removed paper, sorted books and checked them off against the invoices, she wondered about the healthy respect these girls seemed to have for the chief librarian, a respect which almost bordered on fear. Whether they liked him as well as respected him, she had not yet been able to discover, but certainly they did not want to merit his disapproval.

Her attention was caught by some of the books she was handling. A number of them, she found, were so technical and involved that she wondered who could ever be interested enough to want to borrow them. She commented on this and Pearl Matthews heard her.

'Most of those books will have been specially requested by individual readers,' she explained.

Carolyn sighed as she pulled another parcel towards her.

'Fed up already?' Stella asked, laughing. 'After only two days?'

'It's just that the parcels seem endless,' Carolyn said. 'Does this unpacking go on indefinitely?'

Stella nodded. 'We do buy thousands of books a year, so it isn't really surprising.'

They stopped for a short coffee break, then the unpacking went on. Carolyn opened a parcel that was smaller than the others, and as she removed the layers

43

of paper, she judged from their binding that they were old and probably very valuable. Reverently she opened one of them and exclaimed with delight as she saw that it was a study of a famous poet published a hundred and fifty years before.

'If only I'd had this before I took my deg——' She stopped, looked up into interested faces and went on hurriedly, 'for my exams at—at school.'

'Good heavens,' Anne snorted, 'you must have taken school seriously if you worried about your exams as much as that!'

Carolyn could have kicked herself for her slip and knew she would have to be more careful in future. Somehow she must keep quiet about the fact that she was a graduate, then thought how stupid it was that she should feel guilty about possessing a degree.

She sat back on her heels and became completely absorbed in the book. She was not aware of time passing. The chatter, the rustling of paper, all faded into the background as she read the words, and it was not until Anne nudged her arm that she became aware that the chatter had stopped and the whole room seemed to be holding its breath.

Her eyes travelled slowly upwards, from the feet that were standing squarely beside her, on and on to meet two icy, sarcastic eyes. She knelt there, immobile, frightened, flushing deeply, looking up.

'If all my staff did what you were doing, Miss Lyle,' the voice felt like barbed wire rubbing against her skin, 'surrounded by books as we all are, no work would be done at all. So kindly close that book and *get on with your work!*'

As she looked up into Richard Hindon's implacable face, she felt not remorse but anger—that he should speak to her like that, that he should do it in front of the others, that he should make his dislike of her so plain and so public. All her hatred of him returned.

She scrambled to her feet and faced him. She started

to speak, to answer him back in the same tone and terms as he had addressed her. Their wills did battle, the command in his eyes quelled hers and she stammered out an apology. She knelt down slowly and went on with her work.

She knew that every person in that room had been watching them. She felt humilated and beaten, yet he had only spoken a few words. She watched his feet move from her side, heard him talking to Miss Blane. She caught the words, 'Keep her on routine work, labelling, numbering, accessioning only. Don't let her within a mile of the cataloguing.'

Just how nasty could he get? she wondered. He had remembered Mr. Cotes' reference to her interest in the subject and instead of encouraging that interest as he would have done with anyone else, was using it as a weapon against her.

When he had gone, Stella let out a deep, relieved sigh. Anne frowned. 'My goodness, Carolyn, you nearly had it! Much more and you'd have been out—for good. One thing he won't take is anyone questioning his authority.'

Carolyn shook her head. 'I couldn't help it. He gets me that way. I—I just can't stand the man.'

Stella laughed. 'You know what they say, Carolyn, about hate and love being first cousins.'

'*Love*?' Carolyn almost shouted the word. 'How any woman could love him——' She paused. 'I'm sorry for his wife.'

'Wife?' Stella stared at her. 'What wife? Whose wife?'

'Mr. Hindon's, of course. I saw her last night when I was dining with a—a friend. Mr. Hindon was there and his wife joined him. Nice-looking, she was, too nice for him.' She described her.

'My dear, that wasn't his wife, that was his sister. He's not married.'

Anne joined in. 'He hates women, didn't you know?

He's all right to us, but that's because he doesn't see us as women, only library assistants with high-pitched voices!'

The others laughed, and under the cover of their laughter Carolyn tried to ignore the curiously uneven beat of her heart.

'So he's not married? But surely he's got a—a. . . .

'Girl-friend?' Anne shook her head. 'Not one, dear—unless he has a very secret private life no one knows about! Have you met his secretary?'

'You mean Miss Harvey?'

'*Mrs.* Harvey. She's a widow, and a merry one, too. Now there's a woman who'd like to become his friend —a close friend, as they say.'

Stella said, 'Does she turn it on when he's around! Once I went into his room when she was in there, and the atmosphere was *thick*, my dear. And were they working? Not on your life! She was smoking, and they were laughing so much they didn't hear me knock.'

'She's nice-looking,' Carolyn admitted grudgingly, reaching out for another parcel of books.

Stella shrugged. 'Whether you like her looks or not depends on how catty you are. Sometimes he seems to be what you might call—succumbing to her charms. You know, giving in gracefully.'

'Well, she might—just—get him where she wants him one day,' Anne commented, 'but he'll never marry her. He's not the marrying kind. The only thing he's really crazy about is chess.'

Carolyn lifted her head. 'He plays chess?'

'No,' Stella said, 'he doesn't play it, he's above *playing* it! He composes chess problems, something much more difficult, I'm told. You need to be brainy to do that.'

The girls worked on in silence for a while, then Carolyn asked, 'Where does Mr. Hindon live?'

Anne answered. 'With his sister and her husband. He hasn't been here all that long, you know. We heard

46

he was looking for a place of his own, and his sister offered him a room because her husband was going abroad for six months or so. She didn't want to be left in the house alone with her two kids. Bit of a helpless type, I think.'

Stella remarked, 'Rumour has it that they don't get on, but he doesn't like to leave her until her husband gets back.'

'How do you know all this?' Carolyn asked, searching for the invoice among the pile of books she had unpacked.

'Grapevine. You know Miss Stagg?'

'The lady who brought me in here yesterday morning?'

'The same. Bit of an old crow. She's the chief assistant, the deputy librarian's right hand man, sorry, woman, although sometimes, you'd never guess!' She laughed with the others. 'Anyway, she helps Mr. Cotes, and while she's up there, she has a natter with Mrs. Harvey, who passes on all this information—in confidence, of course!—to Miss Stagg, who passes it on—in confidence—to someone else!'

Carolyn discovered that evening that Pearl Matthews lived only a few streets away from her. They caught the same bus home and as they sat side by side, Pearl asked bluntly, 'Have you got a University degree?'

Carolyn turned her head swiftly. 'Yes, but how did you guess?'

'Well, this morning, when you found that book you were reading when Mr. Hindon came in, you just stopped yourself mentioning it, didn't you?' Carolyn nodded. 'So that explains why you came into librarianship later than most of us. Why didn't you get a job in a University library? I would have thought you were better qualified for that.'

Carolyn moved her shoulders as if shrugging off all responsibility. 'My uncle heard of this vacancy so, as it was near my home, I applied.'

She stared out of the window at the houses—Bull-man houses, it registered with her dully—and saw that the trees were flowering in the spring sunshine.

'What I can't understand,' Pearl said thoughtfully, 'is why Mr. Hindon put you in the stock department, and why he's keeping you on such routine jobs. I should have thought that for someone like you— you're four or five years older than girls usually are when they start with us—an explanation would have been sufficient.'

Carolyn looked at Pearl. She was very tempted to tell her the truth. Could she be trusted to keep it to herself? She seemed honest and serious and more responsible than the others. She decided to take the risk.

'Please don't tell anyone, Pearl, but yesterday, when Mr. Hindon called me in to see him, he said—well, you should have heard what he said to me.' Her voice wavered and steadied. 'You know I'm here on six months' trial?'

Pearl nodded. 'All the juniors are.'

'Well, he as good as told me he would do his best to get rid of me within that time.'

Her eyes full of sympathy, Pearl asked, 'But why, Carolyn? You haven't been with us long enough yet to do anything wrong.'

So Carolyn told her the whole story and afterwards, when they were walking home, Pearl said, 'He's ruth-less in some ways, especially about getting his own way. If there's anything in his path, he removes it—we've noticed that in the short time he's been here. He's made lots of changes, some of them much needed, but if you're in his way, and he says he'll get rid of you, then believe me, he will. And there won't be anything you can do about it, or your uncle either.'

Carolyn's voice rose plaintively. 'But suppose I like the job so much I want to stay? And I think I would,

48

given the chance.'

Pearl shook her head. 'That won't make him change his mind. If that's really his attitude to you, then you were on your way out the moment you came in the door.'

Carolyn waved to Pearl as they left each other, and walked the last few yards to her house. What kind of a man is he, she wondered, who could ride roughshod over every obstacle in his path and cast aside so pitilessly everyone who got in his way? Her hatred of him revived and she resented fiercely the almost godlike control he seemed to have over her destiny—and his own.

CHAPTER THREE

HER grandmother greeted her on the doorstep with the usual question on her lips. 'Very nicely, thank you,' Carolyn said in answer to her query. She laughed in what she hoped was a carefree fashion and said, 'I've worked hard, so I'm tired now.'

What she did not tell her grandmother was that she was depressed about what she had just been told and that, if the chief librarian had his way, her days at that library were numbered.

After her meal, she decided to call on her uncle. If she told him that she was happy and that the library was a wonderful place to work in, it might prevent his calling to check up on her. Anything, she thought, to put him off the scent.

Shane opened the door. 'Hallo, darling. How's the big bad boss?'

She frowned and shushed him and he put his hand to his head. 'Sorry,' he whispered.

'Hallo, dear. Austin's away,' Shane's mother kissed her.

'Hallo, Aunt Maisie.' Carolyn followed her aunt into the dining-room. The table was still covered with the remains of the evening meal and Carolyn accepted the cup of tea which her aunt pushed towards her.

She was a well-built woman, determinedly blonde, although around fifty. She was good-natured and placid and had never complained at the amount of money her husband had spent on his niece's upbringing and education.

'He's got plenty,' she would say. 'We won't miss what he spends on you. Or your gran.'

Shane wandered in and poured himself a cup of tea. The house, opulent as it was in furniture and fittings, with an unmistakable 'architect-designed' look about it, had a lived-in air that made a visitor feel at home. Carolyn thought her uncle must like it that way, but even if he didn't there would not have been much he could have done about it, because that was how his second wife ran the home—casually, untidily, but happily.

'How's Donna?' Carolyn asked.

Maisie Bullman, always eager to talk about her daughter, told her in detail what a wonderful time Donna was having in Paris. 'She's not working too hard, and her boss is taking her out a bit, although I think he's a bit old for her.'

'What does that matter?' Shane asked laconically, sipping his tea. 'My sister always manages to enjoy herself, no matter who she's with or where she is. If you put her down in the middle of a lecture on stocks and shares, she'd still manage to enjoy herself, if only by looking at all the men around her and one by one getting their attention off the speaker and on to her!'

They laughed and Maisie said, 'Austin's gone North. Some building conference.'

Carolyn's heart lifted. 'How long for?'

'A few days, dear. He wasn't sure when he'd be back.'

This was too good to be true. He couldn't visit the library while he was miles away in the north! She felt a sense of reprieve and was even able to parry, with some skill, her aunt's inevitable question—how was she getting on in her new job?

Avoiding Shane's grin, she told her aunt how much she liked it, elaborating on the importance of the stock department and embroidering on the mundane duties of the assistants who worked there until it sounded as though the whole building would fall apart without them.

As Shane walked with her to the bus stop—she had refused his offer of a lift—he laughed at her efforts and she felt she had to warn him to be more careful in future about keeping to himself all she had told him.

'I'll guard my tongue like a mother goose watches over her goslings,' he promised. 'By the way, Dad's given me a couple of tickets for some art exhibition by a collection of local artists. It's a private view, prior to the official opening. Like to come with me?'

'Before I answer that question, who's going to be there?'

'You checky imp! Do you want to know if the company will be good enough for you to mix with?'

'Yes,' she said, laughing.

'Well, there'll be the local top people, you know, from the mayor and mayoress downwards, to the intellectual types like the education chief, library chief. . . .'

'Oh,' said Carolyn, 'so he'll be there.'

'Of course, because the art gallery comes under his control. Aren't you coming now?'

If you but knew, Shane! she thought. Now she wanted to go even more. To mix with him socially, even if in full view of the public, to meet him on terms of equality rather than inferiority—the mere thought gave her pleasure.

'Yes,' she said, 'on second thoughts I'll go with you.'

He bowed. 'Thanks for being so magnanimous about it, Madame.'

The bus came along and he helped her on to it and waved as it drove away.

The deputy librarian called into the stock department next day. He walked round the room and chatted with the girls, commenting on how busy they looked. He paused beside Carolyn and she rose to her feet wearily, her boredom and her unhappiness showing through.

Mr. Cotes smiled encouragingly and exchanged a few words with her and went behind the partition to talk to Miss Blane. When he left them, he said he would come again soon.

Stella commented acidly, 'The chief yesterday, the deputy today—why this sudden interest in us, this touching concern for our welfare? They've never given a damn about us before.'

Carolyn stripped the brown paper off yet another parcel and said, 'It must be because I told Mr. Cotes the other day what you said about this department being "Siberia". He seemed quite concerned, so I suppose he thought he'd try to remedy it by coming in and letting us know somebody loves us!'

The short, sharp silence stung her into raising her eyes and looking round. She wondered if she was imagining a cooling of the atmosphere.

'Seems we'll have to mind what we say in future,' Anne snapped. 'Having a V.I.P.'s niece in with us is going to be hard to live up to. Bit like having an intercom permanently switched on—from us to them.'

Carolyn bit her lip. 'I'm sorry about that,' she murmured. 'I'll have to be more careful in future.'

Nobody answered and the silence went on. At one stroke, it seemed, she had made herself an outsider. 'A spy in the place.' That's what they were all saying now, from the chief librarian downwards. She began to wonder how long she could stand it.

That afternoon, Miss Blane called her and the partition cut off the staring eyes of the others. They still had not forgiven her for passing on their 'secrets' and it was a relief to escape from their silent censure even for a few moments.

Miss Blane smiled and invited her to sit down. 'Mr. Cotes thinks you should be transferred to other duties, to something more productive, as he put it, and which made just a few more demands on your intellect!' She laughed. 'Would you like that?'

'Oh, I'd love it, Miss Blane. Something like——' dared she say it? '—cataloguing?'

Miss Blane laughed again. 'Good heavens, no! You'll get round to that eventually, but certainly not yet. No, Mr. Cotes thought you should be introduced to what we call "accessioning". In a library—you've probably noticed it when you've borrowed books in the past—we give every book a number and a classification. Then the books are labelled and we type these details on the catalogue cards. Or instead of typing them we get the cards, already printed, from a central cataloguing agency. These cards are indexed under both subject and author, and we put them into the lending section so that the public can refer to them when they want to find a particular book. We also have a "union catalogue" which contains details of all the books we have in stock in the library.' She turned to Pearl. 'I'll hand Miss Lyle over to you, Miss Matthews. Perhaps you would explain these things to her.'

Pearl gladly put aside her own work and showed Carolyn how to fix to the front page of each book a label. This showed the name of the branch library to which it was going, gave information about the length of time a book could be retained by the reader, warnings about fines and instructions about renewals.

'Take great care with the large reference books you come across,' she told Carolyn. 'Some of them are terribly expensive to buy.'

At the end of the day, Pearl asked her if she was feeling happier about her work, and looked pleased when Carolyn answered, 'Much happier, thanks. I feel I'm getting somewhere now.'

Pearl laughed. 'This is nothing, really.'

'All the same,' Carolyn said, 'it's a lot better than unpacking parcels!'

Carolyn wore her black velvet dress for the art exhibition opening. Its plunging neckline gave her a sophisticated and worldly look and she wondered what Richard Hindon's reaction would be when he saw her in it. It would shake him and it might even shock him, but he would certainly notice her. She twisted her plaits round her head like a coronet and this added to her general air of sophistication.

She felt a little reckless as she sipped her drink and felt Shane's arm round her waist. She waved to her aunt, who was looking attractive in a long white dress. Standing next to her was Austin and he seemed to be enjoying an argument with a fellow alderman. 'So Uncle's home already,' Carolyn thought, her heart sinking.

Where, she wondered, was Richard Hindon? She found him and Roseanna was beside him, staring into his eyes with what she probably hoped was a hypnotic gaze, and appeared to be drinking in his words as though they were nectar. They must have been alcoholic, too, because she swayed, put out her hand and clung to his arm as though she was in need of support. Carolyn watched and could have shouted with laughter at her ingenuous tactics.

Richard smiled down at his secretary and Carolyn felt a stab of something that was surprisingly like jealousy and it turned her expression into a glower. He lifted his head at that moment and saw her. She switched on a brittle and entirely artificial smile. He raised his eyebrows at her provocative look and she flushed and turned away to talk to Shane, who responded with his eyes as well as his words.

'If you look like that the whole evening, sweetie,' he said, 'I won't want to eat the food they've provided. You're so delectable, I'll eat you instead! So beware.' His eyes wandered round the room. 'I'll have to leave you soon to do the rounds. Unfortunately, I have to mix business with pleasure and butter up my prospective and affluent clients of whom,' his eyes took on a narrow, selective look, 'there must be many here tonight.' His gaze stopped short at Richard Hindon. 'Who's that woman with your boss?' Carolyn explained. 'My God, I don't like his taste in females. A widow, you say? Then she ought to know that to catch a man, she should be just a little more subtle in the way she goes about it.' He kissed her cheek. 'I'll join you later, darling.'

She was left standing alone and somehow had to escape from that sardonic look in Richard Hindon's eyes. She searched madly for her uncle and his arm stretched out towards her. 'Carolyn, my dear, meet Harcourt Wesler, artist and sculptor. He's here to open the art show. Harcourt, my niece, Carolyn.'

Her eyes were captured by a gaze intensely blue and penetrating. Her hand was lifted to the artist's lips in a courtly gesture which was strangely at odds with his dress. In spite of his old-world manners, his clothes announced in unmistakable terms that he was strictly an artist in the modern idiom. He spoke with a faint accent.

'Your niece is a beautiful woman,' he said, bowing over her hand and giving it back to her as though it were a delicate and priceless carving. 'And that hair—such colour! It is surely incomparable.'

Her uncle leaned closer to him and said in a stage whisper, 'There's something under that hair, too, I can tell you. Brains. She's got a degree.' He stabbed his chest with his finger. 'I saw to that.'

Harcourt Wesler looked impressed and asked quaintly, 'And now you have it, what do you do to pass the time?'

Her uncle answered for her. 'She's a librarian.'

Aghast at his deliberate exaggeration of her status, Carolyn cried, 'I'm not, Uncle——'

'But that is wonderful.' Mr. Wesler turned and spoke to the man who had joined them. 'Richard.' Carolyn flushed at the chief librarian's sardonic smile. Mr. Wesler went on with a flourish, 'You two have something in common. Allow me to introduce the beautiful niece of. . . .'

'We have met,' Richard remarked dryly. 'Frequently.'

'I'm on his staff, one of his assistants,' Carolyn explained in a flat tone.

'My dear man,' Harcourt put his hand on Richard's shoulder. 'How fortunate to have working for you such beauty and such brains contained in one small—and very feminine—frame. You must surely prize her beyond belief.'

Two blue eyes moved in her direction. 'Indeed yes,' the voice said, soft and subtly caressing, 'Miss Lyle's value to me is beyond estimation.' Only Carolyn could detect the hard glint in those eyes and the cynicism which spiked the too-flattering words.

Austin, believing that the chief librarian was speaking with sincerity, said, 'There you are, my dear,' patted his niece on the back and moved Mr. Wesler on to the next group.

'Carolyn, how nice!' The mayoress, her chain of office moving rhythmically up and down on her ample chest, greeted Carolyn with outstretched hands. The mayor, her husband, followed closely behind and did the same.

'How long is it since we've seen you, Carolyn?' the mayoress went on. 'You've been away, I believe?'

Her husband nudged her. 'She's at University, love. Austin told us.'

'I was at University, Alderman Wilkins,' Carolyn corrected him. 'I've graduated now.'

'Working at something terribly clever, dear?' the mayoress asked.

Carolyn, already acutely embarrassed by the presence of the man beside her, wished they wouldn't make their close acquaintance with her quite so obvious, although she had known them since she was a child.

'I'm working at the library, Alderman Wilkins.' She looked slyly at Richard, and under the cover of the circumstances, dared to say, 'According to Mr. Hindon, in a temporary capacity.'

She heard his short quick breath and knew that for once she had turned the tables on him. When the mayor said, over his shoulder as he moved after his wife, 'Ah, going on to better things, no doubt,' she almost burst into ironic laughter.

They were not left alone. Roseanna sidled up and slipped her arm into Richard's. He allowed it to stay there, but did not move away.

'Delightful pictures, Richard,' she gurgled into his ear. 'Do stroll round with me and look at them.' She pulled gently at his arm, but he did not move.

'I have seen them, Roseanna,' he said quietly.

'And do you like them, Mr. Hindon?' Carolyn asked. 'You appreciate this modern art?'

'In my position, Miss Lyle, and as the art gallery comes within my sphere of influence, it would not do to commit myself in answer to that question. I strive, in art as in all things, to keep an open mind.'

Carolyn, growing bold with the wine she was drinking, opened her eyes to their fullest, most incredulous extent. She hoped he would recognise the reason for her exaggerated disbelief. He did. His expression hardened and he said, softly, so that his companion, close though she was, could not hear, 'An open mind in *all* things, Miss Lyle, including the most junior members of my staff.'

'So you never commit yourself, Mr. Hindon, you never let it be known on which side of the fence you sit?'

'Never, Miss Lyle, not even politically. In my position, it would never do to declare my interests. In this set-up,' he indicated the crowds around him, 'with everyone knowing everybody else, it wouldn't do at all to let one's feelings be known.'

'Oh, Richard,' purred Roseanna, hearing only his last few words, 'don't say that! A man shouldn't hide his feelings, especially where women are concerned.' She clung to his arm and gazed up into his face.

He ignored her, so did Carolyn. They were carrying on a conversation which had nothing whatever to do with anyone else in the room.

'Of course, Mr. Hindon,' she challenged him, 'one first has to assume that you have any feelings at all.'

He took in her half-smile and wide-open eyes. She was not aware that they were over-bright with the drink she had imbibed and that they held an invitation which was as provocative as what she was saying. She knew only that for once she was speaking to him on equal terms and gave no thought to the fact that, in just a few hours' time, their relationship would be back to normal and he would once again be in command.

He looked at her narrowly. 'I assure you, Miss Lyle, that as a member of the human race, I have my share of that commodity called the emotions. That I have better control over them than other people is, shall we say, my good fortune?' He might have added, from his grating tone of voice, 'And, at this moment, yours.'

His arrogance and conceit pricked her into unguarded sarcasm. '*You* have feelings, Mr. Hindon? You surprise me. If you hadn't mentioned the fact, I really wouldn't have noticed. I can only assume they're getting a little rusty through disuse.'

She saw his fingers close over the stem of his wine glass until she thought it must surely break under the pressure. By the look in his eyes, which sparkled with a frightening anger, she knew that before very long she would have to pay for the indiscretions of her tongue. But the fear that gripped her oddly under the ribs was tempered with a sense of triumph that, just for once, if only for a passing moment, she had got the better of him.

Harcourt Wesler, artist and sculptor, took the floor and after a long and largely irrelevant speech—everyone forgave him, explaining away his verbal meander-

59

ings as artistic temperament—he declared the exhibition open.

Afterwards, Carolyn wandered round the room studying the paintings and sketches. She found them puzzling and tried to read some meaning into them.

'Now it's my turn to ask questions, Miss Lyle.' Richard was beside her. 'You like what you're looking at?'

She replied unequivocally, 'No.'

'Why not? Tell me.' He seemed really interested, but she could not put her thoughts into words.

In the end she shrugged. 'Perhaps because I don't understand them.'

'But you don't have to understand them. You don't have to know why the sky is blue in order to enjoy its blueness. You don't have to understand the beauty of a woman's face,' his eyes held hers and his tone had a touch of intimacy about it, 'or the colour of her hair, or,' his eyes lazily took in the provocative plunge of her neckline, 'the attractions of her body, to appreciate them.'

She flushed at his expression and her hand lifted protectively to her throat. He saw the defensive gesture and smiled. She hated his mockery and reproached herself for letting him see how deeply his reactions affected her.

With an effort she recovered herself and, eager to divert his attention away from her, she said, lifting her arm, 'All these are merely expressions of these artists' inner feelings, their hates and their obsessions, the outpourings of their frustrations. There's no harm in their painting them out of their systems, but why inflict the results on us, and then call them works of art?'

His smile irritated her as he deliberately sidetracked by asking her, 'You don't believe in working off your frustrations?'

He was still not taking her seriously. He was laughing at her again and she flushed angrily. 'It depends,' she snapped, 'on the frustrations.'

He grinned. 'A very wise answer, Miss Lyle. Most important to make a distinction.' His smile grew cold and gave way to a scowl. 'Your uncle is after his prey.'

Alderman Bullman stood, head belligerently forward, in front of Richard Hindon. 'You, I suppose, Mr. Librarian, like all this stuff on the walls. Approve of anything, wouldn't you, provided it made a rude noise at convention?'

Richard took this provocation calmly. 'That is not entirely true, Alderman Bullman. I have a healthy respect for all that is old. I have to, because in my job I come across it so often.'

Hands on hips, the alderman did not seem to notice the sarcasm and came back at him, 'I suppose you're talking now about us old 'uns. All right, perhaps we are a bit old-fashioned, but we're entitled to our ideas. Old they may be, but at least they're well tried and well established. Not like yours, so new and weak they've still got their mother's milk on their lips!'

'Without new ideas, Alderman Bullman,' Richard replied, and Carolyn wondered at his continued patience, 'there would be no progress. They have to be given a fair chance. Surely all ideas—even your "old" ones—were new when they were first thought of?'

Austin gave the snort of the vanquished and moved off, muttering with just a little less conviction than before, 'Him and his new ideas!'

A hand fastened on to Carolyn's shoulder and Shane's cheek brushed hers. 'Darling, forgive me for neglecting you, but I've been doing a public relations job. Come with me, sweet. Having you next to me, with all your charm and your—er,—' he looked her over from head to foot, 'other assets, is far more productive than the most expensive advertising campaign.'

Richard, his anger spilling over now that the alderman had gone and his son taken his place, called to Roseanna as though he owned her. She came to heel at once like an expertly trained and devoted poodle. She made a fuss of taking his arm and Richard, without another glance at Carolyn, drew his secretary to the other end of the room.

Drooping suddenly and not even trying to answer the question in Shane's raised eyebrows, she followed her step-cousin round the different groups, responding automatically to their questions, laughing with forced gaiety at their jokes and generally giving the impression of enjoying herself to the full. She did not speak to Richard Hindon again, but she saw him often, Roseanna in tow, talking, laughing and conversing as convincingly as she was. But she knew that whereas his was a true enjoyment, hers was a mere pretence.

The following day, Carolyn hurried through her lunch and returned to the stock room ahead of the others. She searched among Miss Blane's reference books and found the volume she was looking for. Everyone called it 'Dewey' and Miss Blane consulted it every time she classified a new addition to the library. The book fascinated Carolyn and she had secretly made up her mind to attempt a trial classification of her own.

She opened it and leafed through its pages. Then realised she needed a book to classify, she picked one from the shelves at random. The door was opened, but she did not look up, assuming it to be one of the girls coming back from lunch. If the others saw what she was doing, they would probably laugh at her. She turned the pages, becoming more puzzled than ever. Classification was not the easy thing she thought it would be.

'What the devil do you think you're doing!' Her head jerked up and she looked into eyes so cold and so critical that the large, thick book almost fell from her lap.

'Who gave you permission to fool about with Dewey? I gave strict instructions that you should not be allowed within touching distance of cataloguing.' Richard Hindon held out his hand for the book, but she gripped it tightly. 'Give me that book. I will not have you wasting your time when you should be working....'

'This is my lunch hour, Mr. Hindon. We're not usually made to work in our lunch hour.'

'Lunch hour or not, I allow no one, no one *at all*, to fool about with library property, and that includes the chairman's niece.'

The urge to retaliate was too strong to resist. 'Are you one of those librarians, Mr. Hindon, who don't want their assistants to educate themselves and improve their knowledge? Do you purposely underestimate the ability of members of your staff?'

'No, Miss Lyle. I'm as capable as anyone in authority of perceiving intelligence in those I lead, *when* that intelligence exists——'

She interrupted, and in her anger challenged him audaciously, 'Perhaps you go out of your way to choose assistants of mediocre intelligence in order to keep them under and make sure they don't get ideas above their station?'

She was breathing fast and as she looked at him, waiting for his next move, the words she had just spoken bounced back at her like an echo from across a valley. Anxiety took over—what would he say? What would he do? She had defied him and challenged his authority. Would he pick up the telephone, dial that alderman and void her appointment, as he had threatened to do?

His eyes moved deliberately, leisurely, over her face. He said coldly, without expression, 'If you can't show me respect, Miss Lyle, at least show me good manners. However much you may chafe at the idea, I am in charge here.'

She flushed under his keen, quiet gaze. 'I'm sorry,' she murmured, adding bitterly, 'I'll try to remember my place—my very junior place—in future.'

He raised his eyebrows but made no comment, and again held out his hand. 'That book, please.'

This time she passed the book over to him. 'Now the other, the library book you were looking up.' She gave that to him, too.

He walked round the partition and put the book on Miss Blane's desk. 'Come here, Miss Lyle.'

She followed him and he indicated a chair with a movement of his head. 'Bring that next to me and sit down.'

As she settled herself in the chair, he allowed himself a fleeting, sarcastic smile. 'What you might call a little bit of in-service training—something I usually leave to my deputy and my chief assistant. However, I'll make an exception of the chairman's niece.'

She sat, hands clasped on her lap, watching him open the book.

'You know who Dewey was, Miss Lyle? He was an American—Melville Dewey—who, in 1873, invented what is known as the Dewey decimal system. He divided all knowledge into ten specific groups. Each of these groups he sub-divided into ten sub-groups, and so on. Thus, for example, because social sciences are classified at 300, if you take a book on sociology, you'll find it at 301. Understand?' He looked at her and she nodded, the suggestion of a smile easing the tightness from her lips. 'Good. You're with me. Now, if we take a book on—let me think of one—say, on social theory in modern times it's classified as. . . .' he flicked through the pages of Dewey and pointed, 'here it is, 301.15. And so on.'

She cleared her throat, trying to speak naturally to him. 'Do you ever get an awkward book?'

'You mean one that doesn't fit properly into any special category? Certainly. Where's that book you had?' He read its title. 'My word, you chose a difficult one. You would!' He smiled and it transformed his face. Her heart gave an odd jerk as she smiled back. 'It's about the Somerset and Dorset railway.' He opened it. 'M'm. Seems it dates from Victorian times. Now, since it's about steam engines, it could be classified as engineering, in which case its class number would be—er—621.13.'

'Oh.' A short sigh of relief escaped her, as though a difficult problem had been solved.

'Ah, but——' he raised his hand, 'it's also about transport, in which case its class number would be 385.3. Or is it rail engineering? That would make it yet another number. You see what I mean when I say that classification can be a difficult and tricky business, and that it's best left to the experts?'

She nodded. 'How do you become a cataloguer, Mr. Hindon?'

He watched her fingers playing with the bows on her plaits. 'By passing your exams, Miss Lyle, and by specialising in it from the start.'

'Oh.' Her face fell.

'Not an impossible task for someone with the necessary interest—and intelligence.'

She looked up at the word and saw the mockery in his eyes.

'Which I haven't got.'

He closed the two books and stood up. 'That, Miss Lyle, remains to be seen. Now I'd better go before the others come in and think I've taken leave of my senses.' He stopped in the doorway and looked at her. He said softly, 'I'm beginning to think so myself.' He closed the door behind him.

CHAPTER FOUR

IT was the end of the day and all the others had gone. Knowing that her grandmother would be out for tea —she had gone to visit her sister who lived a train journey away—Carolyn had stayed behind to finish some work.

Now, with a sigh, she closed the stock-department door behind her and stood for a moment, looking about her. She could feel the stillness of the deserted library, the almost macabre silence of the great, museum-like vastness of the lending section, with its books stacked into the brown wooden shelving. Shadows, grey and mysterious, slanted down from the roof-high windows, and the flavour of the last century was everywhere. It must, at times, have made the chief librarian despair.

All the same, Carolyn felt growing inside her a sense of belonging to the place and a determination to do everything in her power to be allowed to stay there.

She turned away from the entrance doors and gazed up to the top of the stairs. What was up there, besides the chief librarian's office and his deputy's room? The words 'Reference Section' were painted on the wall in large black letters. She glanced at her watch—just time, she decided, to look round it before the librarian in charge went home.

She ran lightly up the stairs and followed the directions which led her to two glass-panelled doors. She pushed them, but they would not yield. They were locked. She was too late. Disappointed, she turned back and saw Mr. Cotes standing in his doorway.

'Hallo, Miss Lyle. Did you want something from there?'

She was confused. 'Oh no, it's all right, thank you. I

just—wanted to have a look at it, that's all. It doesn't matter.' She went past him, but he put a hand on her arm.

'Wait a moment. Haven't you been shown round? No?' He frowned. 'Not even the children's library? We'll have to remedy that. It's our usual practice to show all newcomers round on the first day.' He went into his room. 'Have you a few minutes to spare?'

'Yes. That's why I came up, but everyone's gone.'

'Then I'd better do the honours. Just a moment, I'll get the keys.' He opened a drawer and took them out, said 'Follow me' and went towards the reference library.

As they passed the chief librarian's room the door opened and Richard Hindon came out. His secretary was hovering in the background.

'Hallo, Richard,' Mr. Cotes said, 'I'm just taking our new member of staff on a sight-seeing tour. Did you know she hadn't been shown round the building?'

Richard Hindon seemed to take the omission personally. His eyes flickered unpleasantly. 'I'm sorry I've fallen down on my duty and failed to recognise Miss Lyle's V.I.P. status. Accept my apologies, Miss Lyle, for failing to observe protocol in your case.'

Roseanna Harvey sniggered. Mr. Cotes looked upset and rested his arm protectively on Carolyn's shoulder. Carolyn smouldered at Richard Hindon's calculated insult. She said, through stiff lips,

'There are times, Mr. Hindon, as you may know, when I don't recognise protocol myself, so I can hardly expect it in return, even if it applied to me, which you know very well it doesn't. All I ask is the normal politeness which would be shown to any other member of your staff.'

Roseanna drew in her breath. Mr. Cotes' hand tightened momentarily on Carolyn's shoulder, then fell away. 'Here's a girl,' he must have thought, 'who needs no protection.'

But if his hand had remained a few seconds longer, he would have felt her body tremble as she took the full brunt of the look that Richard Hindon flung at her.

Roseanna smiled at Mr. Cotes. 'Richard—I mean Mr. Hindon—is giving me a lift home, Mr. Cotes.' She switched her gaze to Carolyn and her lips parted with something which was not so much a smile as a silent cry of triumph. She slipped her arm into Richard's, looked coquettishly at Mr. Cotes, and gave her escort a gentle tug. Like a lamb, he walked away beside her. 'Do come in and have a drink with me,' they heard her say in a loud whisper as they went down the stairs.

It was an hour before Graham Cotes locked the heavy entrance doors and followed Carolyn down the steps to the pavement. She thanked him for showing her round.

'Thank you for bearing with me.' He looked over her head at the passers-by. 'You'll be going home now, I suppose? Can I offer you a lift?'

'That's very kind, but I can get a bus.'

'I should like to give you a lift. I've nothing else to do. I'll take you home with pleasure.'

They walked round to the library car park. He smiled at her. 'I suppose you've got a date?'

'Not tonight. I think I'll have a lazy evening.'

He stood still. 'I suppose I couldn't persuade you——?' He walked on uncertainly. 'No, I couldn't, of course I couldn't.'

He stood still again, looked at her hopefully. 'But—would you? Would you come out for a meal with me?'

Carolyn began to refuse, saw the hope in his eyes begin to die, smiled and said, 'Well, it's very kind——'

'You will?' he broke in. 'That's fine, that's good. Now, where shall we go? Somewhere quiet?'

The restaurant they chose was tucked away in a side street. 'I'll leave the choice to you,' Carolyn told him as he studied the menu. Covertly, while his attention was diverted from her, Carolyn looked at him. There was a loneliness about him that seemed to cling like another layer of clothing. There was more grey in his hair than his years merited and she wondered about him, thinking how pleasant he was and how different from the man he worked with.

He gave the order and said, with a smile, 'I suppose you've got an inexhaustible list of boy-friends?'

'Not really. I go out with Shane, my uncle's stepson. We're friends.'

'Only friends? And you an attractive young woman? Surely not!'

'Oh, I don't take Shane seriously, any more than he takes me. Another girl's only got to look at him in a certain way and he's off on her trail, nose to the ground!'

They laughed. He said, casually, 'So you're heart-whole?'

'I—I——' The hesitation puzzled her as much as him. She stamped the seed of doubt into the ground and said, positively, 'Of course.'

Their food arrived and they began to eat. She asked him. 'How long have you been working at the library?'

'Oh, more years than I care to remember. I've moved progressively upwards in status. Now I've stopped.' She looked at him enquiringly. 'I drew the line at the top job, so I didn't apply for it. I'm not the type to take permanent overall control. I know my limitations. In that, as in—er——' he looked at her and looked away, 'other things.'

He fiddled with the cutlery. 'I'm forty-one, only four years—calendar years—older than Richard. But in experience, I'm twenty years older.' He looked at her. 'My wife died—I suppose you heard? We'd only been married a few years.'

'You've never remarried?'

He shook his head. 'Never wanted to—so far.'

She ventured, 'Mr. Hindon—he's not married either.'

'Richard?' He made a face. 'He's got a heart somewhere inside him, but it's so deeply embedded I doubt if any woman will ever penetrate that far.'

'What about Mrs. Harvey?'

'Not her. She's backed the wrong horse.' He laughed. 'But he keeps her on a string and does it so cleverly, she thinks it's the other way round. He doesn't want to lose her—she's a darned good secretary. She understands his funny ways.' He said, hesitantly, 'I'm sorry about the chief's attitude to you, Miss Lyle.'

She took a breath to answer him, but the words caught in her throat, and she choked back a curious desire to cry. She shook her head instead. 'It—it doesn't matter,' she managed.

'But I imagine it must hurt.' She shrugged, trying unsuccessfully to look as if she didn't care. 'That library is his life,' Graham went on. 'He's absolutely determined to lift it out of the rut it fell into under his predecessor. His ideas are so far ahead of his committee's that he frets when he finds they aren't with him.'

'And my uncle's the worst of them all, I suppose?'

He avoided the question and said, 'The trouble is, Richard won't work within the system. All the time, he's wanting to break away, to push ahead and out distance them. Anything—anyone who holds him back, he becomes impatient with.'

'I know. And I, as the chairman's niece—I'm sacrificed with all the others.'

'That seems to be it, I'm afraid. You see, Richard's dream is a new library, purpose-built and furnished, with modern equipment, shelving, lighting, ample storage space, the lot. But the money just hasn't been forthcoming.'

They talked about other members of staff. 'Have you made any friends yet?'

She told him about Pearl Matthews. 'Ah now, Pearl,' he said. 'She's one of the best. But she needs to break away from home. She's too comfortable there, too dependent on her parents.' He smiled. 'She should find herself a boy-friend and get married.'

'That seems to be every man's remedy for every young woman's ills,' Carolyn laughed as they left the restaurant and walked to the car park.

Graham took her home. He thanked her for her company and drove away, a hand raised, a smile on his face. She hoped, as she watched his car turn the corner, that she had eased his loneliness just a little that evening, and somehow it made her happier to think that she had.

'Carolyn, we need you.' Stella took her arm when she arrived next morning. 'Look at all those parcels. A new consignment of books just arrived, all for unpacking.'

Miss Blane came round the partition. 'Leave the labelling, Miss Lyle, and give them a hand this morning, will you?'

They were still working feverishly towards the end of the afternoon. There seemed no end to the books. Each one was checked against the invoice, stamped with the name of the library to which it had been allocated, and pushed into the bookshelves to await accessioning. As the shelves filled up, Carolyn knew that she would be labelling and numbering the new additions and filling in cards with the books' details until she could see them in her sleep.

She was on her knees admiring a particularly costly atlas when the door opened and someone spoke her name. She knew who it was and could hardly breathe for fright. Her uncle stood there, his size filling the doorway, his eyes taking in with unbelieving horror his niece's position, her occupation and her apparent fear.

'What's this?' boomed Alderman Bullman. 'Scrubbing the floor?' It wasn't a joke, it was never intended to be. It was a declaration of war on the man behind it all. 'And how long has this been going on?'

At his belligerent tone, Miss Blane crept round the partition and quaked at his wrath. 'I'll see about this,' he thundered. 'Where's Mr. Librarian Hindon?'

'In his room, sir,' Miss Blane quavered. 'I'll take you to him.'

He waved her aside. 'I know the way. I'll see about this, Carolyn, my lass, I'll see about this!'

He swung round and Carolyn called to him. 'Please, Uncle, don't——'

But he had gone. She attempted to follow, but sank back on to her knees. For a despairing moment she covered her eyes, feeling the pity of everyone in that room. Even so, as she looked round at them all, there seemed to be a barrier, a withdrawal on their part of the comradeship they had offered her since she had started to work there. Suspicion made them turn their heads away and Stella gave her a 'whose side are you on?' look which made her want to hide her eyes again.

She hardly spoke for the rest of the afternoon. Miss Stagg came in, her eyes seeking Carolyn out, and slipped behind the partition.

There was a mumbled, 'My dear, you should have heard him! We could hear every word. I don't know what the borrowers must have thought. It made me quite ashamed, his booming voice shouting all about his precious——' A quick intake of breath as a hand covered a mouth.

It was time to go and still the summons to the chief librarian did not come. Pearl's sympathy on the way home helped a little and her falsely bright chatter stopped Carolyn's mind from dwelling on the feelings of the man who had been at the receiving end of her uncle's tirade.

Her grandmother asked as she went in the front door, 'Did you see your uncle today? He rang to say he was going to see how you were getting on.'

'Yes, Gran.' She nodded wearily. 'I saw him.' She left it at that.

After tea her uncle walked in. He threw himself into an armchair, every inch the successful master builder, with a dash of the respectable alderman thrown in to add colour and flavour.

He began at once, 'Well, I had a proper set-to with that man Hindon, my dear, and I've put it right for you now.' He snorted. 'My niece down on her knees! I've never heard the like. I gave it to him straight from the shoulder.'

Carolyn winced, wondering what was coming next.

'She's my niece, I said. I won't have her doing the jobs of a servant girl. On her knees unpacking parcels, sticking on labels! Why, a half-wit could do that. And what d'you think the young puppy said? "She's not qualified to do anything else." Why, man, I said, she's got a degree. Of course she's qualified. I didn't spend all that money on her education for nothing. Then what did he say? "Her degree's irrelevant." *Irrelevant!*'

'But, Uncle, it's true. He's right. I'm not qualified. You need proper training and have to pass exams to qualify for librarianship.'

But Alderman Bullman was not listening.

'So while he was on the run, I tackled him about choosing new books for the library. Why haven't we been given a list of books to choose from lately? Then he said in his damned high-handed way, "I've abolished the book sub-committee." I nearly exploded, I can tell you. "It came into existence," he said,' and her uncle mimicked derisively the chief librarian's cultured tones, ' "to help my predecessor. I don't need that sort of help. Under my guidance," he said, "the books for this library are selected on a wider basis. I consider readers' suggestions. I consult my branch librarians

73

and my senior staff. I also allow my junior assistants to have their say—even your niece, Alderman Bullman," he said.' Austin slapped the arm of the chair.

Carolyn could imagine the smile on Richard Hindon's face as he had said that.

'Even my niece!' Austin persisted. '"You're putting my niece on the level of a *junior*?" I said.'

'But, Uncle,' Carolyn protested, 'he's right. Of course I'm a junior.'

Austin twisted his head on his thickening neck and stared at her. 'Whose side are you on, girl, I'm beginning to wonder? That young puppy's—or your uncle's?' Carolyn didn't answer. 'You know which side you bread's buttered, lass.'

'He's right, dear,' her grandmother urged. "You must take your uncle's part, after all he's done for you.'

Moral blackmail, Carolyn thought bitterly, the tug of the puppeteer on the strings. And I'm the puppet, I have to do as I'm told, or else . . . I'm the butt between them. I'm the football they're kicking around, each trying to get the better of the other.

'I'll teach him who's boss,' her uncle muttered as he left, 'even if it kills me. I'll stop him at every twist and turn so much that he'll realise in the end he can't beat us. Then he'll just have to join us! You see, he'll finish up an Establishment man like the rest of us. Him and his new ideas!'

Miss Stagg greeted her as she went in the entrance doors. 'Mr. Hindon wishes to see you as soon as you arrive, Miss Lyle, so you'd better go straight up.'

Here it comes, she thought, taking off her coat and holding it over her arm. The match of the day's begun. How many goals will he score off me—as many as my uncle did? She trod slowly up the stairs, wondering how he would greet her.

His secretary stood at his side, one hand on his

shoulder, the other holding a shorthand pad. Her greeting was a smirk, her expression condescending and amused. But he didn't even raise his eyes.

'I'll let you know when I'm leaving, Mrs. Harvey,' he said. She nodded and went to her room.

His eyes remained down. 'Take a seat, Miss Lyle.' His tone was long-suffering, weary even. His hands shuffled the papers in front of him into some sort of order. Suddenly he looked up, his eyes narrow.

'Tell me, Miss Lyle, why did you get your uncle to confront me as he did yesterday? Didn't you have the courage to come and see me yourself?'

She caught her breath, taken completely off guard by his attack.

'Why do you want a change? Do you consider yourself above that sort of work? Think it's an insult to your intelligence, perhaps, a waste of a good degree to put you on to such routine tasks? Is that why you got your uncle to force my hand? Are you not being treated with sufficient deference—not enough red carpets out?'

She flushed at his words, then her fire died down and went out. It didn't even smoulder. What was the use? She couldn't fight two men. She couldn't even fight one any more.

She said, with effort, 'I didn't ask my uncle to see you. He came of his own accord. Whenever he has asked me how I've been getting on here, I've told him how much I like it, how—how happy I am,' her voice wavered, but she brought it under control. 'I haven't let you down. I have some loyalty to you as my superior, although you, of course, will choose not to believe it.'

'Thank you for those few kind words.' His sarcasm burned her, his imperviousness to her appeal distressed her. It was impossible to get through to him, but somehow she had to make contact.

He went on, 'Nevertheless I've had my orders and as

I'm at the mercy of the library committee, I have to do as the chairman of that committee tells me. So, like a pawn in a game of chess, I shall have to move you. But from now on I play it my way. You understand that?'

She nodded. She gripped her hands on her lap and met his eyes. He immediately withdrew his and found a pen to fiddle with.

'Mr. Hindon, I'd relieve you of my presence if I could. If it were in my power, I wouldn't hesitate, I'd leave. I know you don't like me and don't want me here,' He stirred impatiently. 'But I've got to stay. You see, it takes great strength of mind to break away from a certain set course—a course which has been decided for you by pressure of circumstances, by a sense of obligation to the person who has mapped out that course for you.' She wondered if he was listening. 'It takes determination and—and courage. You probably don't know what I'm talking about. You've probably been a free agent all your life, living as you want, choosing your own career from the start and pursuing it single-mindedly until you reached the top. Well, you're lucky, Mr. Hindon.' He lifted his eyes to hers, saw the appeal, the pleading in them for his understanding, and looked down again.

'You're luckier than you know.' She hesitated, wondering when he was going to stop her talking. But it looked as though his mind was hardly on what she was saying. He had taken his ball-point pen to pieces and he seemed at a loss as to how to put it together again. 'You've probably never been burdened with the good intentions of someone else, or with a feeling of obligation so strong that it inhibits your thinking and makes you powerless to control your own destiny.'

The pen was starting to fit together, but it came apart again when she said, in a voice he could hardly hear, 'I'm torn in two, Mr. Hindon. I have my—my loyalty to you, because you're the man I work for. But I have my loyalty to my uncle because of his generosity to me since childhood.'

He looked up. 'You have no parents?'

'No, I live with my grandmother. My mother died years ago, and I haven't seen my father since I was five.'

At last the pen was all in one piece. He scribbled with it on his blotter to make sure it worked, then he flung it down on to the desk. 'I'm visiting one of our local branch libraries. You'd better come with me. We usually take our new members of staff to see the branches. Is that your coat? You'd better put it on.' He glanced out of the window. 'It's raining.'

He walked round the desk and helped her put on her coat. He took one of the waist-length plaits in his hand and asked with a kind of masculine detachment, 'What do you do with these things?' He saw her questioning look and added, 'In the rain, I mean. Do you just let them get wet?'

'No, I put them under my coat.' She took the plait from him and their fingers touched. She snatched hers away as though she had been bitten by a dog. He appeared not to notice and held the door open for her.

They left the building by the rear entrance and as they got into his car he asked, 'Do you drive?' She shook her head. He started the engine, switched on the windscreen wipers and drove towards the main road. 'No? Your uncle's slipped up, hasn't he?' The sarcasm was there again.

'Since it's unlikely that I'll ever have a car, what's the use?'

He was concentrating on the road. 'Can't your boy-friend teach you?'

'Boy-friend?'

'Yes, the one I saw you dining with the other evening.'

'Oh, Shane. He's my uncle's stepson.'

'M'm. He seemed capable of teaching you a thing or

77

two.'

She flushed. 'I take exception to that!'

He shrugged and drew up at traffic lights. 'Take it how you like.'

So he was still taunting her, even now he would not leave her alone and treat her like any other human being.

The lights changed and he drove on. They passed a park and a newly-built public hall. 'Bullman Community Centre', it was called. She saw him glance at it, then throw a quick look at her. She glared at him, daring him to say a word about it, but he merely smiled mockingly and remained silent.

He changed gear and turned a corner. 'My sister is looking for a baby-sitter. She saw you the other evening and thought you would make a good one. She goes round assessing everyone for their baby-sitting potential. It's a sort of disease she suffers from. Anyway, she thought you had the right kind of face, one you could trust.' He gave a short cynical laugh. 'I said that was a matter of opinion, but in any case I told her she couldn't ask the chairman's niece—and a University graduate into the bargain—to look after her kids.' He negotiated a tricky road junction. 'She said no, she couldn't, but I could.' He halted at a pedestrian crossing and stared ahead. 'I'm only mentioning it because otherwise I should be landed with the job myself. And that I could not stand.'

Her heart was behaving curiously as she asked, casually, 'Don't you like children, Mr. Hindon?'

'Not particularly. I don't seem to have the paternal instinct.' He flicked her a glance. 'And don't look at me as though I were a leper. Since it's an absolute certainty that I'll never have any of my own, it doesn't matter, does it?'

She thought, so he's not even human in that respect. Aloud she said, 'I'd like to baby-sit for your sister. I love children.'

78

'You do? I suppose when you get married you'll have half a dozen?'

'No. Three will do very nicely.'

'No doubt there's some fool of a man around who'll be willing to oblige.'

'I wouldn't marry a man who didn't love children, Mr. Hindon.' As she realised what they were talking about, she flushed again.

He was frowning and said in a flat tone, 'I'll give my sister your answer. I'm warning you, though, you'll have to take what's coming to you. And I mean that. I know my sister's kids, only too well.'

He drew up in front of a building which could have been called an architect's dream. Each side of it was shaped like a wedge of cheese, the roof being dipped and sloping to a point near ground level. The walls seemed to consist almost entirely of windows and the whole effect was one of invitation to the onlooker to go and see what it was like inside.

Richard Hindon got out and told Carolyn to follow. He strode ahead of her, pushing through the swing doors and holding them open for her to enter. The girl at the counter, a short trim blonde with a bright smile, greeted him with unconcealed pleasure.

He introduced Carolyn briefly, then disappeared with the assistant into a room which opened out of the lending section. Carolyn didn't like to follow. She wandered round, looking at the books, noting the modern design of the shelves and the clarity with which each section was marked. There were low tables which displayed new additions to the library and colourful posters on the walls. The whole place had a lively feeling about it which contrasted strongly with the sombre, repressive air of the central library.

There were only a few borrowers wandering round making their choice and Carolyn walked across to the counter where the books were date-stamped. She heard voices from the office.

'We'll give her some training,' Richard Hindon was saying, 'then could you absorb her here? It would relieve us of her. . . .' The assistant must have protested, because he lowered his voice. 'I know it'll be a bit of a burden because she won't be fully trained, but don't worry, it will only be for a short time. She doesn't stick at anything for long.'

Her face flamed and she caught at her bottom lip with her teeth. So that was what he thought of her—a burden, a relief to get rid of. Her shoulders sagged. What did it matter? She had to accept the inevitable. 'If he said he'll get rid of you,' Pearl had said, 'then he will.'

He came out of the office, said goodbye to the assistant and called to Carolyn to join him. 'Well,' he said as they drove away, 'did you learn anything from your visit?'

'Yes, thank you,' she answered steadily, 'I learnt a little about my future place of work.' He looked at her sharply. 'I heard what you were saying about me,' she said dully.

'Once again.' He shrugged. 'Well, if you will go round eavesdropping. . . .'

She bit back the retort she longed to make and said, 'All the same, it's a wonderful building.'

'It certainly is.' He became talkative. 'It's only recently been opened. I chose the fittings and furniture myself, soon after I came. It's my dream—a central library like that but on a much larger scale. A purpose-built construction with plenty of space, windows everywhere, modern fitments and lighting, everything functional.' He laughed shortly and repeated, 'It's a dream of mine.'

'I know. Mr. Cotes told me.'

'Oh? When?'

She hesitated. 'I—er—had a meal with him the other evening.'

'Really?' For some reason there was cynicism in his

tone. 'Fast worker, Graham. Or an opportunist.'

She tightened up. 'Must you reduce everything to the lowest common denominator, Mr. Hindon?'

'Yes, Miss Lyle,' he answered blandly, 'where you're concerned. After all, why do you think I'm telling you about my "dreams"—only because I hope you'll pass them on to your revered uncle. I'm attempting to exploit to the full your so-called "loyalty" to me.'

Her fingers gripped the edge of the dashboard. 'If we weren't near our journey's end, Mr. Hindon, I'd—I'd. . . .'

He broke in with a grin, 'You'd get out and walk?' He pretended to be upset. 'What? Has the chairman's niece taken a dislike to me?' He tutted. 'We can't have that.' He drew up in a parking space. 'After all, she might use her influence in the right quarter and get me dismissed.' She slammed the car door and he was still smiling broadly as he got out. He joined her and dropped his baiting tone, becoming once again the man in charge.

'My sister will contact you about the baby-sitting.' He turned. 'I'm going in the back way. You'd better go round the front. You'll be working in the lending section from now on. One of the senior staff will show you what to do.'

She went slowly towards the front entrance feeling oddly lost without him. She wished he hadn't left her. Then she pulled herself together and convinced herself she was glad he had gone.

Miss Stagg detailed a senior assistant to be her instructor in the lending library. He was a tall, high-spirited, red-haired young man. His name was Keith White, he said, as he shook her hand.

'I see we have something in common.' He was eyeing her hair. 'Only they obviously put more colouring mater into mine. But,' he touched her plaits, 'they must have given you some powerfully strong growing agent.'

She laughed, liking him immediately.

'Now, where shall we start?' They began with introductions to all the other members of staff. 'Section heads,' he told her, 'are in charge of their own particular departments—children's section, lending and reference sections, stock department and so on. Then there's Miss Stagg. She's just a little higher in the hierarchy. Lower down there's us, the lesser fry, the senior assistants. We're general dogsbodies. We do research work, indexing, compiling booklists, and we attend to readers' requests. We also act as readers' advisers, sitting over there at that table marked "Enquiries". Last of all there are your lot, junior assistants, you do the routine stuff that doesn't require much intelligence.' She laughed at his expression. 'But you'll learn all about it as you go along.'

There were two girls at the central counter. They introduced themselves as Sandra and Cathy and showed her how to date-stamp the labels and take the card from the book and put it into the readers' tickets.

Some libraries, Keith explained, were very up to date and used a method which microfilmed the record of the transaction. This, he told her, cut down the queues at the counter, which was a good thing, especially on Saturdays, which were always very busy. This method also allowed the assistants to work sitting at a desk. It was an expensive way of doing things, but it was Mr. Hindon's aim one day to install it. Another of his dreams, Carolyn thought. Would any of them come true?

'When you're not on counter work,' Sandra said, 'you'll have jobs like sorting through books which need to go to the binders for repair. Another job is sending letters to readers with overdue books. Every morning when you come in, you'll be given a section of shelving and told to tidy the books.'

Keith asked, 'Are you any good at lettering? If so, you might be allowed to have a go at poster work for display in the library.'

'What happens to out-of-date books?' she asked as they walked along the shelves.

'We take them out periodically and put them away in a special store. We daren't part with them for years. We may think they're too old, but you throw out a book on, say, the phonograph or crystal wireless sets—a little before your time, I think!—and next day someone will come along asking for information on the subject. So we have to be very careful.'

After lunch, Pearl slipped out of the stock department and asked Carolyn how she was getting on.

'I love it,' she told her. 'I hope Miss Blane wasn't too annoyed about my transfer. It wasn't my doing, Pearl. I hope you all realise that.'

'I do, Carolyn, but Miss Blane was a bit upset. You see, most people stay in our department for six months!'

Keith beckoned Carolyn towards a door which opened off the main library. 'Here's the store room for the old books. This is a very ancient one on the teaching of chemistry, but we dare not part with it. Any time a mythical Mr. Smith from the oldest established school in the town might come along and ask for it to help him prepare his notes, because he doesn't hold with these "new-fangled" modern methods of teaching!'

They were laughing when Mr. Cotes walked in. 'Hallo, Miss Lyle, you sound happy.'

'Oh, she is,' Keith said. 'She's found a soulmate in me. After all, look at the colour of our hair.'

Mr. Cotes pretended to frown. 'Now I call that an insult even to talk about Miss Lyle's hair in the same breath as yours.'

'Oh, I don't know.' Keith seized a long golden plait and wound it round his neck. As he was so tall, this brought his face down close to hers. 'There's a certain similarity.'

Mr. Cotes picked up the other plait and examined it

closely. She was caught between the two men and laughed helplessly.

'Miss Lyle!' Richard Hindon stood at the door.

The laughter stopped abruptly, and even Mr. Cotes looked embarrassed.

'What the devil's going on in here?'

'Sorry, Richard,' Mr. Cotes' voice was placatory. 'It wasn't Miss Lyle's fault.'

'That may be your opinion, Mr. Cotes. It isn't necessarily mine.'

Graham Cotes pursed his lips and walked out.

'Mr. White,' Richard Hindon was addressing Keith, 'in your position as a senior assistant, it's your job to keep juniors under control. Kindly make sure that this girl is kept under control in future.'

'Sorry, Mr. Hindon.' Keith looked abashed. 'It was my fault entirely.'

'That is not *my* opinion, Mr. White.' He gave Carolyn a scathing look and went out.

Carolyn spent most of the next few days sorting books for repair and pushing trolleys round replacing returned books on the shelves.

One morning Miss Stagg called her to her desk. 'Mr. Hindon wishes to see you at once, so leave whatever you're doing and go straight up.'

Carolyn sighed. Now what had she done? She was growing accustomed to the feeling of dread she always experienced on approaching the chief librarian's door. She knocked nervously and went in. The receiver was resting on the desk, and Richard pushed it towards her.

'My sister wishes to speak to you. I told her it's highly irregular to call a junior member of staff to my office to take a phone call, but she insists on speaking to you personally.'

Carolyn said into the receiver, 'Carolyn Lyle here.'

'Oh, Miss Lyle,' the voice was a little gushing, 'I'm

so glad to have a word with you. I'm Richard's sister. You might remember seeing me at that hotel the other week.'

'Yes, I remember, Mrs.——?' Carolyn looked enquiringly at Richard, but he kept his eyes on his work.

'It's Mrs. Roding, actually, but please call me Hilary. You're Carolyn, aren't you? Well, Carolyn, my brother told me you were terribly kind and said you would baby-sit for me.'

Hilary Roding was speaking so loudly, Carolyn had to hold the receiver some distance from her ear. 'That's right, Mrs.—er—Hilary.' Richard Hindon's eyebrows rose a fraction but he still did not look up.

'Well, my dear, would you be free this evening? Or have you got a date?'

'Yes, I have tonight. I'm sorry.'

'Would it be with that gorgeous hunk of man I saw you with the other evening?'

Carolyn laughed. 'Yes, he's my step-cousin, Shane.' Tired of standing upright, she looked round for a chair, but it was too far away to reach so she bent down slightly to rest her hand on the desk top. Her plaits swung forward and one of them brushed Richard's cheek and came to rest on the paper he was reading. His sigh was protracted and long-suffering and he picked up the plait between finger and thumb as though it was a playful kitten and lifted it to one side.

When Carolyn saw what he was doing, she snatched the plait out of his reach and stood upright. She caught the remnants of an irritating smile and turned her back on him.

'My dear,' Hilary went on, her voice carrying round the room, 'I thought he was quite dishy. Are you going to marry him?'

Carolyn laughed again. 'Well, I—I really don't know. We haven't discussed marriage yet.'

She heard a furious scribbling and turned to see the chief librarian writing with some viciousness on a piece of paper. He pushed it across to her and pointed to it. She read, 'Tell my sister to get off the line and let you get back to work.' He was glowering at her and she said apologetically into the telephone, 'I really must go in a moment, Mrs.—er—Hilary.'

Hilary laughed. 'I suppose my brother's telling me off for babbling. Well, all right, I'll get to the point. Could you baby-sit tomorrow evening?'

'I'd be pleased to—er—Hilary. What time shall I arrive?'

'Oh, eightish will be fine, and I shouldn't be back too late. Some friends are having an evening do—you know, drinks and things. I'll see you tomorrow, then? Now could I have a word with my brother?' Richard, who could hear, shook his head.

'Sorry, but he says "no".'

She laughed. 'Tell my dear brother that he's as much an old fuddy-duddy as those councillors he's always complaining about. 'Bye for now.'

Carolyn put the phone down. Richard Hindon shook his head like someone who had given up hope.

'All I can say, Miss Lyle, is that you're an even bigger fool than I thought you were.'

She answered politely, 'Thank you for those few kind —and flattering—words, Mr. Hindon.'

She watched as his eyes opened to their fullest extent, then walked out.

CHAPTER FIVE

'HALLO, Carolyn.' It was lunch-time and Graham Cotes, with Richard following close behind, caught her up on the library steps. 'Where are you off to?'

'For a quick swim. It's such a lovely day.'

He put his hand on her arm. 'What, going hungry? No lunch?'

'Oh, I've got sandwiches.'

He called over his shoulder, 'Wish I could come with you,' and hurried after Richard.

Carolyn spread her coat on the sand and opened her hold-all wide. With her towel wrapped protectively round her, she took off her clothes and dropped them into the hold-all. It took only a few minutes to pull on her two-piece swimsuit. She wound her hair round her head and pushed it into a tight-fitting cap.

Trying to avoid the larger pebbles, she tiptoed to the water's edge, flinching slightly from the chill breeze. She stood for a moment hugging herself and inhaling the sea-fresh smell. Apart from one or two people stretched out on the sands snatching half an hour's sunbathing before returning to work, she was alone.

From the shore the sea looked limitless, the horizon hazy and mysterious, while yachts and small craft rocked with the gentle movement of the waves. Taking a deep breath to give herself courage, she ran into the cool waters and did not stop until she was completely immersed, then she rose and swam. She struck out from the shore, growing tired after a while. She turned on to her back and floated, watching the wisps of cirrus clouds in the blue depths of the sky.

She became aware of the passing of time and remembered her sandwiches. An hour for lunch wasn't long enough on a day like this. She wanted to linger in the water, but with a sigh waded to the shore and ran lightly up the slope of the beach to her belongings.

She tore off her cap, shook her plaits down over her shoulders, rubbed herself lightly with a towel and without bothering to remove her wet swimsuit, took out her sandwiches. Contentedly eating, she watched the gulls in their swooping unpredictable flight and listened to their passionate cries.

The sun was drying her swimsuit and she undid her plaits, took out a comb and ran it through the waist-length hair. She turned her head to push it out of the way down her back when her eye was caught by some-one lying a few yards away. He appeared at first sight to be sleeping. His hands were supporting his head like a pillow and his face was turned towards her. He was not asleep. His smile, broad and mocking, told her that.

A slow flush crept up her neck to her cheeks and she tore her eyes away. So Richard Hindon had followed her there. He must have heard her telling Graham where she was going. He must have had his lunch—her eyes sought the high white stone frontage of the hotel she knew he patronised—and had come down to the beach just to annoy her.

How was she going to take off her swimsuit with him so near? She panicked. The towel—she grabbed it and made a clumsy effort to unfold it when she heard a movement at her side. He was looking down at her, a goading half-smile on his face.

He said, 'However seductive the weather—and you —may be, Miss Lyle, time, alas, passes.' He looked at his watch. 'When you've finished behaving like a pro-vocative mermaid, I'll give you a lift back to work.' She drew in her lips to make a stinging reply, but he went on, 'If necessary you'll have to leave the plaiting of those golden tresses until you get in the car. I can't have a member of my staff late on duty because of vanity.'

She nearly took up a handful of sand and threw it at him, but he moved away a few yards and sat down, rested on his elbow and watched her. The towel went round her this time and, pink with embarrassment and exertion at having to dress so quickly, she struggled beneath its folds, glaring now and then at the cause of her predicament.

Taking the hint at last, he smiled, stretched himself out complacently on the sand and closed his eyes. Or she hoped he had. At last she was fully clothed, and somehow he seemed to know this—his eyelids must be transparent, she thought petulantly. He stood up, hands in pockets, still watching her.

'I must comb my hair,' she snapped, and he looked at the time again and shrugged. She willed him to go away, but he stood his ground, lazily contemplating her as her hair crackled and hissed through the teeth of the comb. With swift experienced fingers, she made two long plaits, tied the bows and stood up. The sand fell away from her and she brushed her skirt and legs, gathered up her belongings and told him she was ready.

They did not speak on the way back, and the silence was taut and uncomfortable and cried out to be broken. If I were anyone else, she told herself miserably, he would probably have talked non-stop. Because it's me, he dries up like a garden in a drought.

She thanked him, without gratitude, for the lift.

'Next time,' his voice was dry, 'you'd better keep better track of the time. Otherwise you might get into trouble with the boss.'

He smiled maddeningly as she slammed out of the car and ran into the library.

Hilary Roding flung the door wide open. 'My dear Carolyn,' she said, 'I really am delighted to see you. Now we can introduce ourselves properly.' They shook hands. 'I tried to get my brother to introduce us that evening at the hotel—he goes there every night for his meal, you know, says he can't stand my cooking—but he absolutely dug his heels in and refused.'

'Are your children in bed?' Carolyn asked.

'Yes, but the little horrors won't settle down until they see you. Come in here for a moment. Let's get acquainted. How do you like working under my char-ar-ming brother?' Her voice drawled sarcastically. 'It must be hell. Is it?'

'Well, I—I——' But Carolyn was saved the agonising necessity of answering, because Hilary went on,

'Carolyn, my dear, your hair, what a glorious colour. And my dear, the length! It must have taken years to achieve that.'

'Yes, it has——'

The front door opened and banged shut. 'Ah, there's my dear brother now. Come in, Richard. I've got a charming young lady with me. Not that you ever see a woman as a woman.' She grinned at him as he stood at the door. Carolyn's heart was beating pain-fully fast as she raised her eyes to his. Somehow she expected to find censure there, but there was nothing, no expression at all.

'Good evening, Miss Lyle,' he said, and turned to go.

'Richard, I've just been telling Carolyn what won-derful hair she's got. Don't you agree?'

'I—er. . . .' His glance ran over her face and down the plaits. 'Yes,' he said flatly as if answering simply to keep his sister quiet.

'I think she's quite beautiful. And my dear, how well that outfit suits you. I wish I could wear slacks as well as you do. With a figure like yours anything would look good, even an old sack.'

'I thought she came to baby-sit,' her brother said dryly, 'not to have drooling compliments thrown at her.'

He left them and as he went upstairs to his room, his sister said, 'My brother can be so unpleasant at times.'

Carolyn thought wryly, 'You can say that again!'

Hilary went on, 'He needs a good woman to humanise him. All the same, I'd feel sorry for any woman he took a fancy to.' The door was open and her voice was deliberately raised. 'If she ever put her arms round him she'd get as much response as she'd get from an iceberg. Less, perhaps. At least an iceberg melts a little when warmth is applied to it even if it doesn't possess any internal heat itself! Even if he had central heating installed inside him, it wouldn't warm him up. His emotional temperature still wouldn't rise above zero.'

A door slammed upstairs. Carolyn asked, 'Has he never had a girl-friend?'

'Oh, good heavens, yes, he's had a few affairs, but they've all left him cold.' She lowered her voice. 'His secretary's making a beeline for him, haven't you noticed? But if she thinks she can pot and seal him like a jar of home-made jam, then she's much mistaken. There's not a woman born who can catch him with his barriers down. Now, my dear, let's talk of pleasanter things. Tell me about this fabulous stepcousin of yours.'

So Carolyn told her briefly about Shane.

'Estate agent, is he? My goodness,' she laughed, 'I must start looking for another house soon and become one of his clients.'

'Why, does your husband want to move?'

'No, my dear,' the idea obviously amused her, 'my husband will agree to whatever I want. He's abroad at the moment, did you know? He won't be back for another four months. It's a long time,' But she didn't look as if the fact upset her greatly. 'You know, I'll have to give a party soon and you can bring your young man, then I can meet him.'

Carolyn wanted to remind her, gently, 'But you're a married woman, Hilary. Doesn't that count for anything?'

There was a cry from upstairs, a prolonged and

irritable 'Mummee-ee!' 'Hilary,' another voice thundered down, even more irritably, 'Helen's calling. Are you deaf?' A door was banged shut.

'Coming, Helen darling,' Hilary called to her daughter, 'and I'm bringing your nice new baby-sitter with me.'

Two sturdy pyjama-clad legs greeted them at the top of the stairs and above them was a fair-skinned, flaxen-haired six-year-old, with her mother's self-confident extrovert manner.

She was prettier than her mother, though. She had a delicacy of feature which must have been inherited from her father's side of the family, because her mother did not possess it, attractive though she was.

'Hallo, Helen,' Carolyn said, holding out her hand. She knew the child was sophisticated enough to acknowledge her formal gesture in the orthodox way, and she did. Her hand was small but firm in Carolyn's, and stayed there while the intensely blue eyes—which Carolyn thought vaguely she had seen somewhere before—studied her face.

'What's your name?' Helen asked, removing her hand after the examination was over. Carolyn sensed that she had passed her test with honours.

'Carolyn, Carolyn Lyle.' She touched the short fat plaits that skimmed Helen's shoulders. 'Now isn't that strange we've both got them!'

'Yes,' said Helen, 'but aren't you lucky to have such long ones! How did you get them so long?'

'Oh,' laughed Carolyn, 'I kept on pulling them till they were as long as I wanted.' The child's eyes grew wider. 'I didn't really, you know. They just grew.'

A shriek of annoyance made Hilary dive towards her son's bedroom. 'Darling,' she said, 'we haven't forgotten you. Here's a nice lady to look after you.'

The little boy was chubby and blue-eyed and full of the vigour of a two-year-old. At first he would not look at Carolyn. He hid his face in his mother's dress as she leaned over the bars of the cot, but at the sound of Carolyn's soft voice, he gradually extricated himself and stared at her.

There, she thought with a profound shock, was Richard Hindon in miniature, with all the arrogance and challenge and thrust of his uncle, but in minute proportions.

'Oh, he's beautiful,' she said to Hilary. 'He's a darling.'

She wanted to put out her arms and hold him to her, and she didn't know why. Instead she kept them clasped in front of her and said, 'What's your name?'

He hid in his mother again and muttered something. 'He says it's Basi. It's really Basil, but he leaves off the "l" at the end. So we all call him Basi. To him you'll probably be Caroly, without the "n". Darling,' this to her son, 'Carolyn's come to look after you while I'm out.' He shook his head coyly, but he straightened and stared at her again, this time with less hostility.

His mother settled him down and as she leaned over to cover him with the blankets, he seized her pendant and pulled at it with some force. Hilary shrieked and he let go, but he was laughing so much he curled up under the bedclothes.

'He's an imp,' she said, kissing him, 'just an imp.'

'Uncle Rich calls him a little devil,' Helen offered, behind them.

'He would,' Hilary said. 'He's abusive to anyone who gets under his feet.'

In time, the children were in bed and quiet and Hilary left for her evening out. 'I'll be back about elevenish, Carolyn. That all right? Will your grandmother mind?'

Carolyn assured her that her grandmother went to bed early and invariably slept right through till morning. 'She's marvellous that way. She never worries about me.'

'Oh, good,' said Hilary. She waved, got into her little

car and drove away.

It was peaceful when she had gone, like the calm after a whirlwind. Carolyn roamed restlessly from one room to another. She admired the furnishings, looked at some delicate china in a glass-fronted cabinet, inspected the watercolours on the walls. She went through the kitchen into the garden, feeling chilly now in the evening sun. The garden scents were mixed and fragrant and the fruit trees displayed their blossom with pride.

She walked slowly back and involuntarily her eyes lifted to an upstairs window. She felt as though she was being watched, but there was nothing up there to prove it.

She went inside, switched on the television and left it on, although her mind was not on it. It kept creeping away to a room upstairs where a man was sitting alone. She wished he would make some noise just to prove he was there.

At last she switched off the set and raked in her hold-all for the book she had brought with her. It was a textbook which Mr. Cotes had lent her on library administration and filled in a lot of background which she needed to know.

She was nearing the end of the first chapter when a stifled shriek had her petrified with fright. She flung down the book and chased up the stairs and threw herself into Basi's room. He was jumping up and down in his cot and shouting his head off.

'What's the matter, darling?' she cried, putting out her arms, but he dived away and threw himself full-length on the covers.

'He's only trying you out,' a small, self-possessed voice said behind her. 'There's nothing wrong with him really. Is there, Basi?'

He yelled louder and managed some tears this time. 'Mummee,' he sobbed. 'Want Mummee.'

'He doesn't really,' his sister said. 'It's only because

94

you're new and he wants to see what you'll do.'

Carolyn stared nonplussed at the little girl, and realised with a shock where she had seen those blue eyes before. They were her Uncle Richard's eyes. The man was everywhere in this house. She couldn't escape him.

'Are you sure, Helen? He seems in pain.'

'You heard what my very intelligent niece said, Miss Lyle.' The terse voice came from behind her and she swung round. 'She knows the boy better than you do.'

By this time Basi was standing at the cot rail again, laughing.

'You scamp,' Carolyn said, laughing with him and putting her arms round him. 'You delightful little baggage!'

He tolerated her arms for a moment, then grabbed one of her plaits and pulled. He held on with all his strength and would not let go. Carolyn bit her lip with the pain.

'Uncle Rich,' Helen said, 'Basi's hurting her.' But Uncle Rich stayed where he was, in the doorway with his hands in his pockets. 'Uncle Rich, *do* something!' But Uncle Rich did not move. Basi tightened his hold and Carolyn lifted her hands and tried in vain to free herself.

Tears of pain were filling her eyes, when she heard a sharp, authoritative, 'Basi, *stop it!*' But still the boy hung on. A few short swift strides brought the man in the doorway into the room. 'Stop it, you little devil,' he breathed, and prised the child's fingers away. 'These ridiculous plaits!' Carolyn felt a last vicious tug at her hair which she knew had not been inflicted by the boy, and she could not stop the tears from overflowing now.

'You've made her cry, Uncle Rich,' the high-pitched voice accused him. 'You've made Carolyn cry. You're very naughty.'

Carolyn knew she had to control herself and could not give way to the overwhelming desire to run away and sob for the rest of the evening. She raised her eyes and did not hide her tears.

As she looked at the man beside her, she felt the breath go from her body as though she had been hit by a car. She knew that all she wanted in the world was to be taken in those arms that were now resting nonchalantly against the doorway and be held by them until the pain had passed. She realised with the deepest horror that she was in love with the man and that there was not the remotest chance that he would ever return that love.

'If you're fool enough to take on baby-sitting, Miss Lyle,' Richard Hindon was saying, 'then you take all that goes with it. You're not paid for putting up your feet and watching television. If I were you, I should ask my sister for danger money. Where this little devil's concerned, you need it.'

She glared at him, her eyes glittering with tears, her lips trembling, astounded by his callousness. 'Little devil,' he dismissed him, this beautiful, lovable child. Couldn't he see himself there? Couldn't he see that the boy was the image of him? Couldn't he love him a little just for that?

'Basi love Caroly,' the little boy said, putting out his arms. 'Basi tiss Caroly.' Contrite now, sincerely so, he gave her a smacking kiss on the cheek.

'You've obviously passed his test, severe though it was,' a dry voice came from behind her, 'with flying colours. Congratulations.'

The mockery passed over her now, because she had the little boy in her arms, the boy who was so like his uncle. 'Go to sleep now,' she whispered. 'Sleep, Basi.'

And he curled up into a bundle in his cot and dutifully closed his eyes. Richard had disappeared into his room. Carolyn took Helen's hand.

'Come on,' she said, 'bed now for you, darling.'

She kissed Helen's cheek and she smelt of talc and freshly laundered nightclothes. She was too grown up for Basi's intriguing baby smell. She settled her into bed and crept down the stairs and sank, exhausted, into an armchair.

To stop herself thinking, to hold off the inevitable contemplation of all the aspects and implications of her hopeless love, she switched on the television again. But it was no use. She didn't see a thing.

She made herself some coffee, wondering whether to offer any to the man upstairs. She decided against it and was carrying her cup into the lounge when he came down and passed her in the hall. There was not even a flicker of recognition in his eyes.

Some time later, Carolyn looked at her watch. 'Hilary should be home soon,' she thought, putting down her book and closing her eyes.

She awoke with a start. Someone was speaking her name. She looked at the clock. It was past midnight. She looked at Richard, standing in front of her flicking through her book.

'Going to sleep on the job, Miss Lyle?' His cynical smile got her brain going again and she stood up, unsteady with tiredness. 'I shall have to report you to my sister as unsatisfactory.'

'Is she back yet?'

'No, she's not back yet. Did you really expect her to be?'

'Elevenish, she said.'

'You can always safely add anything up to two hours on to her stated time. That's something you'll learn— *if* you come again.'

She held out her hand. 'May I have my book, please?'

But he did not hand it over. 'Are you trying to impress me by reading this? Where did you get it from? It's not library property.'

'Mr. Cotes lent it to me. It's his own copy.'

'Graham did, did he?' He eyed her and went on softly, 'Well, well. What goes on between you?'

She flushed. 'I don't know what you're implying. But whatever you're thinking is wrong, quite wrong.'

'I suppose you know he's nearly twenty years older than you? And that he's a widower?'

'Yes, he told me. But there's nothing, absolutely nothing between us.'

'On your side, maybe not, but on his....' He eyed her again and she began to feel as though she were on sale at a cattle market. 'He's too nice a man to be fooled around with. I don't care a damn about your feelings, but he's had too much pain in his life to be made to suffer again.'

Pain? she thought. She knew she couldn't bear the pain in her own heart at that moment.

'I hope you've told him your affections are otherwise engaged?'

'Don't worry, Mr. Hindon, he knows all about the state of my affections.'

'So it's got that far, has it?'

'I don't know what you mean.' Her voice rose shrilly in her efforts to convince him.

Abruptly he handed over the book. 'Get your coat, Miss Lyle. I'm taking you home.'

'No, thank you.' She sat down.

'Do as you're told.'

'I'm not going home. I've contracted to do this job and I'm going to see it through. I'm staying until your sister gets back. Anyway, we can't leave the children alone.'

'It won't hurt them for ten minutes. I'll lock up. If they're yelling when I get back, I'll pacify them somehow.'

'I'm not going, Mr. Hindon.' She stood up and they faced each other.

'You're an obstinate little cuss, aren't you?' He lounged against the fireplace and assessed her in a slow, calculated way. He watched with interest as her colour rose. 'Even at this time of night. If you're wor-

98

ried about being paid, there's no need. I'll see you get the money even if I have to pay you myself.'

She felt she could have slapped his face. 'Is that all you think I worry about? Financial reward?'

'It's what is in most young women's minds these days. I'm sure you're no different. You've certainly got a wealthy boy-friend.'

'Well, I'm sorry to disappoint you,' she had to be angry, otherwise she would have cried, 'but it's my conscientiousness that's keeping me here, not any desire for money.'

He narrowed his eyes. 'We'll postpone this very interesting discussion of your character until another time. Just now I'm taking you home. I'm not going to have an exhausted and irritable member of my staff present herself for work tomorrow—no,' he consulted his watch, '*this* morning, so you can stop playing the unbelievably efficient baby-sitter and get your coat.'

She knew she had to obey. She took her jacket from the hall cupboard, glanced uneasily up the stairs, listened intently, heard nothing, and told him she was ready.

He came into the hall and his eyes flicked over her. She knew the droop of her eyelids gave away how tired she was, and she turned from his gaze. He saw the action, which was childlike in its effort to hide something from him, and he made a movement towards her. He must have had second thoughts because he stopped, selected a key from the collection which he took from his pocket, held it out and said, 'Let yourself into the car. I'll lock up here.'

Startled by the almost friendly gesture, she took the key and did as he had told her. She sat for a moment in the driver's seat and ran her hands over the steering wheel, trying to get the feel of it. She groped in the darkness for the handbrake and gear lever and reached out with her feet for the foot pedals.

'Is this a hint that you want to learn to drive?'

She jumped violently at the sound of his voice and moved across quickly to the passenger seat.

'If I taught you to drive I'd bite your head off more than I do now. And you wouldn't like that, would you?' She was sure he was smiling, actually smiling! 'But I guarantee you'd be a damned good driver by the time I'd finished with you.'

She answered in a small, tired voice, 'I don't want to learn to drive, thank you.'

He gave a short unbelieving laugh. Too tired to respond, she let her head rest on the side of the car. But it was not only tiredness that made her head droop sideways. Now it came upon her, wave after wave, like a storm-driven sea, the self-reproach that she had let it happen, the hopelessness of her love, her blindness in not seeing it coming and getting out before it was too late.

He seemed to know the way to her house and he drew up outside. All the road was in darkness, except for the street lamps. She sat silent for a moment, then in a weary voice said, 'Goodnight, Mr. Hindon. Thank you for bringing me home.'

But somehow she couldn't move. 'Are you so tired,' the words were soft and almost caressing, 'that you want me to carry you in? Surely baby-sitters are made of sterner stuff than that?'

She couldn't tell him that her legs felt so strange that she could not be sure they would support her to the front door. She got out and, without turning back, walked unsteadily up the path, found her door-key and let herself in. Only then did she hear him drive away.

Hilary phoned next morning while Carolyn was having her breakfast. 'I'm so sorry about last night,' she said. 'Richard told me to apologise, but you know how it is, those evenings go on longer than you think and you don't like to be the first one to break up the party.

100

My dear, they wanted me to stay overnight!'

'What time did you get home?' Carolyn asked. 'Just so that I'll know what's coming next time.'

Hilary laughed. 'One o'clock. My brother told me off. But I knew he'd be there even if you'd had to go.'

Carolyn smiled at the careless way Hilary had assumed that somehow she would have found transport to take her home so late at night.

As soon as she arrived at the library, she was summoned to the chief librarian's office. Her heart sank. She asked herself the inevitable question—what had she done now? Richard didn't even invite her to sit down. He took some money from his wallet and held it out to her. Like a child being offered cash by a fond relative, she put her hands behind her back.

Roseanna Harvey stood next to him with a slow knowing smile on her face. 'What's that for?' she asked slyly. 'For services rendered?'

Richard's face did not flicker. Carolyn swung her eyes round to the secretary and glared. But she gave up, realising that she could not win against such a fixed, cunning grin.

'For heaven's sake take it, Miss Lyle. My sister sent it. I'm not the donor. I'm merely the messenger. It's for the baby-sitting.'

'Well, that's a new name for it,' said Roseanna.

'Mrs. Harvey,' Richard Hindon turned an ice-cold expression towards his secretary. 'I shall call you when I'm ready.'

Even Roseanna looked abashed at his **tone** and melted away into her own room. 'Now, shall we start again?' He held out the money. 'My sister realises this is in excess of what you agreed between you, but asks you to accept it, with her sincere thanks.'

'It really doesn't matter,' Carolyn said, but she knew she had to take it. 'It's very kind of her.'

'Before you go, Miss Lyle,' Carolyn turned at the

door, 'here's a book which might help you. It's mine. It's better than the one Mr. Cotes lent you. The language is less technical and it's easier to read.'

Carolyn's hands stretched out to receive it as if it were a bouquet of flowers. He was actually lending her a book, on librarianship too! Did that mean he had accepted her?

'That's very good of you.' Her eyes shone into his.

He smiled slightly. 'I shall expect an improvement in your work.'

She smiled back. 'Implying that it needs improving?'

'There's no doubt about that,' he answered, pulling a pile of letters towards him and dismissing her by the action.

Carolyn's uncle phoned that evening. Her grandmother handed her the receiver. 'He wants to know how you're getting on, dear.'

She had to be honest with him. 'I'm loving it, Uncle. I've been on counter duty today.'

'So if I take a book back I might find you there to stamp it for me?' She heard the broad grin in his voice. 'Glad now, lass, I got you off that other job? Never heard the like, Austin Bullman's niece down on her knees unpacking parcels!'

Shane arrived after tea. 'Coming out, darling? I thought of going to a show.'

Carolyn shook her head. 'Definitely not, I'm not in the mood.' She looked out at the bright evening. 'I wouldn't mind a walk.'

He made a face. 'My feet weren't made for walking. But you win. Don't suggest the Downs, though. I couldn't face that.'

She had a vision of the sea and the sand. 'The beach.'

He looked surprised, but agreed. 'All right, I'll indulge your whims for once.' They called goodbye to Carolyn's grandmother who waved from an upstairs window.

The beach below the esplanade was deserted except for a handful of people out for an evening stroll or taking their dogs for a walk.

Shane took Carolyn's hand as they went down the stone steps to the sands. 'Not far off high tide,' he said, as they stood at the edge of the waves.

'My feet are hot,' said Carolyn. 'I think I'll paddle.'

He stared at her. 'And I think you're crazy.'

She moved a few yards back, sat down and removed her shoes. Shane sat beside her and laughed, 'How old are you? Twenty-two or two?'

She stood up and faced him. 'If I were two, you'd have to come to the water with me and hold my hand.'

He laughed and stretched himself out, grumbling about the pebbles pressing into his back. 'No, thanks. You wash your feet. I'll rest my work-weary limbs.'

She looked up at the esplanade, hoping no one was watching. She noted with relief that it was almost empty. There was a man up there, leaning forward against the sea wall, and he was staring out to sea.

She stiffened. She knew who it was even before she saw his face. His eyes seemed to be searching the horizon and there was in his expression something so lonely, so lost and so infinitely sad that an unbearable compassion took hold of her and she wanted to run to his side to offer him comfort.

He had not seen her and she was glad. She dropped down beside Shane, but her very movement had attracted the man's attention. As she glanced up at him again, she saw that the sadness had gone. There was, instead, a rigidity about his body and a hardness in his look that told her exactly what he was thinking.

'What's up?' Shane asked, stirring and rising slightly. He followed her eyes. 'Ah, the big bad boss himself. Aren't you going to paddle now in case he has you on the carpet tomorrow and tells you off for unseemly behaviour?'

His taunt made her defiant. Yes, she had been afraid —for a moment. But not any more. She sprang up and ran towards the sea, shrinking a little from the stones which dug into her bare feet.

She went into the cold soothing water ankle deep, then in a little further and felt the waves wash up and down her legs. She bent down and feathered the water with her fingertips and hoped that by the time she turned to go back, that silent cynical figure would have gone.

Shane wandered down and told her to come out. 'It's getting dark, sweetie, didn't you know? Time little girls were in bed.'

'Has he gone?' she asked over her shoulder.

'No. Your boss is still there. There must be something about this bit of beach that keeps his attention riveted here. Come on, I'll hold your hand on the way back and keep him at bay if he decides to attack.'

So she gave him her hand and he walked her back to where she had left her shoes. He threw himself on to the sands and offered her his handkerchief. 'Dry your feet with that. I'll cherish it for evermore if you do.'

'Don't be an idiot, Shane,' she laughed, trying to forget the eyes that seemed to be piercing her back.

'Yes, I am an idiot. I ought to ask you to marry me. You're beautiful and intelligent and a delightful companion.' He leaned over and kissed her lips.

She drew back at once. 'Don't do that!'

'Why not? I've done it before. Afraid of what the boss will think? Perhaps he's gone.' He looked round. 'No, he's sticking to us like a limpet. What can we do to get rid of him?' He pushed her down and kissed her. She struggled, freed herself and sat up, her heart pounding with anger. She turned wildly. Had he seen?

He was walking slowly into the dusk, eyes down, hands in pockets, with only his loneliness to keep him company.

CHAPTER SIX

NEXT day things went wrong from the start. She was on counter duty. She had been working for some time when she noticed to her horror that she had turned the date stamp to the wrong day. She told Sandra what she had done. Miss Stagg overheard and tutted and shook her head.

Then Carolyn demanded the payment of a fine on an overdue book which the borrower declared he had renewed by telephone. He began to argue and Miss Stagg sent Keith White across to sort things out.

Richard Hindon came in. He stood next to the group, listening. The reader, flattered by such attention, and pleased to have the chief librarian himself there to complain to, declared all over again that he was innocent of everything Carolyn was accusing him of.

Richard looked at her coldly. 'It's time you admitted your mistake, Miss Lyle, and apologised.'

'I'm sorry, Mr. Cranley,' she said to the man, 'I really am. But I'm new to this, you see, and I didn't really understand the procedure.'

But this only made matters worse because, when the man had gone, Richard turned to Keith and said, 'Don't, under any circumstances, allow this girl anywhere near this counter until she has learnt the whole procedure by heart. I can't have her upsetting readers again.'

'I'm sorry, sir,' Keith said, 'but I'm sure I told her all about renewals.'

Carolyn glared at him but he was looking at the chief librarian with such subservience that she felt disgusted with him. *She* wasn't going to treat Richard Hindon with such deference.

'I'm sorry, Mr. Hindon,' she said, wishing the headache that was coming on would let her be, 'but I admitted it was a mistake. Everyone makes them some time.' She nearly added, 'Even the chairman's niece.'

Miss Stagg brought up reinforcements. 'She's been stamping books with the wrong date this morning, too, Mr. Hindon,' and she tutted again.

Carolyn glared at Miss Stagg, but she might have been staring at a statue for all the effect it had on her. What was the matter with everyone this morning? she wondered. Why were they all after her blood like a pack of hounds after a miserable little fox?

She moved back to allow Miss Stagg to pass in front of her and knocked over a pile of books. They went skating across the floor. Everyone in the vicinity turned and stared. Carolyn dived to gather up the books before the chief librarian could even begin to tell her off. They all walked away and left her to it.

She put the books into a neat pile and looked round. Had Richard gone? No, he was still there. Keith came over and whispered with a grin that the chief had given instructions for her to go on shelf-tidying duty. 'He thought that was just about within your capabilities, and simple enough for any fool to do without making a mistake! You surely can't put your foot in it there, can you?'

'No,' she whispered back, 'but I'm going to have a darned good try.'

She ran into the shelter of the shelves like a fugitive escaping into a forest. There she would be safe from any prowling tiger might try to scent her out. She started on the non-fiction section, noting automatically the classification numbers on the bindings.

She moved along the shelves, pulling out books and pushing them back into their correct positions, and reached the section which included books on chess. The word in itself was sufficient to conjure up frightening images of Richard Hindon and she moved on hurriedly.

106

But something drew her back. With nimble fingers she drew a book from the shelves. Her knowledge of the game amounted to little more than the moves of the individual pieces and she turned the pages trying to fathom the strange phraseology and follow the diagrams with their code-like lettering and cryptic numbers.

She felt an odd prickling all over her, as though someone was watching her closely. Like a creature at the receiving end of a tiger's spring, she tensed for flight. She looked into the eyes of the hunter and gave a noiseless cry of terror. She had been caught in the act again and could only stand there and wait for the kill.

He moved to her side. He said, so softly that it was almost a whisper, 'So once again, Miss Lyle, you are committing the unpardonable sin of reading while on duty.'

She held her breath. Was this the end now? Was this what he had been waiting for, watching for, a crime sufficient to justify his contention that she was unsuited to a career in librarianship? Now would he throw her out?

She tried to apologise, but the words wouldn't come. He held out his hand for the book. She gave it to him. He read the title and she dared not meet his eyes. He shut the book and she looked up. He was smiling and she could not believe it. He was smiling, and it was a smile of genuine amusement.

He whispered, 'Remind me to lend you a book on the subject. In time you might even be good enough to play against me. Now,' his expression and his tone returned abruptly to normal, 'get on with your work!' She did.

Later that day, she was pushing a trolley round the library when a reader touched her arm.

'I wonder,' the lady said, 'if you could help me. My grandson's ill and he's fed up with doing nothing. He wants a book and he's sent me to get one.'

'Oh dear,' Carolyn said, immediately sympathetic, 'what sort of book—fiction or non-fiction?'

The lady didn't understand, so Carolyn tried again. 'Has your grandson any hobbies?' She suggested the first thing that came into her head and cursed herself wholeheartedly later on. 'I mean, like—like chess, for instance?'

'Oh yes,' said the lady, fastening on to the word. 'Chess. I'm sure he'd like one on chess. But it would have to be easy book, so he can understand it.'

Carolyn began to wonder what she had let herself in for. What did she know about chess? Then she thought of Richard Hindon. He would be able to advise this lady on a book about chess.

It didn't occur to Carolyn, as it should have done, that she might be breaking library rules by dialling the chief librarian's extension on the internal telephone. Nor did she stop to wonder if she should be consulting him about anything so lowly as the selection of a book. She forgot that he might be annoyed, she forgot about everything except that, for the first time ever, a reader had asked for her help and that help she was determined to give.

First she got through to his secretary, then came an abrupt, 'Yes?'

His tone did not put her off, nor did the long, ominous silence after she had explained her request. Would he come down and help this lady? she asked again. It was a beginner's book she probably needed because.... She chattered on, trying to fill in the empty silence from the other end.

Then there came an explosion in her ear. Didn't she know, he asked crisply, that it was not his job to advise readers? That it was his job to administer the place, not make suggestions? That, in other words, he was above that sort of thing now, that he was not there to wait on people, whoever they were, *not even the chair-*

man's niece?

'What is the Readers' Adviser for, if not to do just that—advise? That's his job, not mine.'

'The trouble with you is,' she stormed, forgetting her place, forgetting his status and forgetting her manners, 'you're so out of touch with life—real life—that you can't get down to the level of ordinary people any more. You shut yourself upstairs in an ivory tower, deaf and blind to everything that's going on down here, refusing to mix with the general public....'

She was cut off by his icy tones. 'That will do, Miss Lyle. Tell the reader in question that I shall be down.'

The receiver was slammed into place. Sober now and aware of the cold hard light of day, Carolyn walked across to the lady who, with her lined face and compassionate eyes, reminded her of her own grandmother. 'Mr. Hindon is on his way,' she said.

Then she grasped the trolley and raced with it to the farthest corner of the library. If she had had the power, she would have crawled on to the shelves and hidden away between the largest volumes until the man in charge had swept upstairs again.

She heard his quiet voice assisting the old lady. He was gentle and helpful, and satisfied her at last with a book on chess that seemed to delight her with its simplicity. 'Why,' Carolyn heard her say, 'even I can understand it!'

He laughed with her, stamped the book himself, which delighted her even more, and saw her off the premises. 'That's good,' Carolyn thought, 'he's in a good mood.' But she changed her mind quickly when she heard, heavy footsteps doggedly seeking her out, treading round the floor, moving between the shelves and probing deep into the corner where she was cowering, half out of sight.

'Miss Lyle,' the voice breathed, 'come—out—of—there!'

As the command jerked from him, she inched her

head from between the trolley shelves and, still crouching, gazed up at him, silently pleading for forgiveness like a child caught in the act. But he was not to be placated.

He snapped, 'Come up to my office.' There was no getting away from him, she had to go.

She followed him all the way upstairs and he faced her across his desk. He was breathing hard. 'Let's get this straight. If I have any more cheek, rudeness and downright bad manners from you, you will be out—out of this building faster than you have ever moved in your life. And what is more, you will not come back.'

'But, Mr. Hindon,' she faltered, 'I only wanted to help the reader——' The tears were marshalling in her eyes like an army, but, powerful weapons though they were, they did not halt his attack. He disregarded them and went on,

'I will not have such brazen impudence from any member of my staff, let alone you, despite your University degree, despite your privileged position, and despite your close acquaintance with some of the top people in this town. You will be out! You understand?'

She used anger to reinforce her tears. 'All right,' she blazed, swept by an uplifting sense of self-sacrifice, 'sack me. That's what you've always wanted, isn't it— to get rid of me? So it's an opportunity not to be missed. I've given you justification now. I've challenged your authority.' The tears spilled over as she waited for her dismissal. 'Go on,' she urged, 'why don't you sack me?'

He didn't move, he didn't even speak.

'All right, I'll give you your heart's desire. I'll hand in my notice and sack myself.'

His eyes narrowed as he counter-attacked. 'I knew you wouldn't stick it,' he jeered, deliberately turning the tables on her. 'Your life must be littered with abandoned projects. First teacher training, now this.

It's yet another challenge you couldn't meet, isn't it?'

She saw then how it would seem to him, and to others, if she gave in now, and she knew he had won.

She started sobbing. 'And all because I wanted to help an old lady.' Her voice was thick and muffled by her damp handkerchief. 'You know so much about chess, you were the first person I thought of. I thought you'd want to help her, too.'

There was a strange silence, then she heard a movement and felt a hand under her chin. He lifted her face and looked into her eyes. The tears were running down her cheeks.

He said softly, 'You can stop playing the martyr, Miss Lyle, and you can stop plucking at my heartstrings. The game's over and the result is stalemate. You can get back to your work now.' He returned to his desk. 'But before you go, you'd better dry your tears. The members of the public—the public you're so fond of—might think you've been reading a very sad novel.'

She gave a watery smile, found a clean handkerchief and proceeded to mop up.

Roseanna edged round the door. She seemed by her gloating grin to have heard most of the conversation. She tiptoed across to the desk. 'I must apologise, Richard. It was my fault really. I shouldn't have put her call through to you, should I?'

Carolyn expected him to reprimand her and say, 'Of course you shouldn't,' but instead he smiled and said, 'I'm not entirely blameless myself.' He looked at Carolyn, still despondent in front of him. 'As soon as I heard who it was, I should have put the receiver down.'

Pride straightened her sagging body. She drew in her lips, met his challenge with defiance and slammed the door behind her.

It was the end of a disastrous day. Carolyn searched in

her hold-all for the book Mr. Cotes had lent her. She hoped he was still in his office. She tapped on his door and he opened it himself.

He looked surprised. 'Aren't you homeward bound, Miss Lyle?'

'Yes, but I thought I'd return your book first.' She put it on his desk.

'I hope it was helpful and filled in some of the gaps?'

'It certainly did. Thanks for lending it to me.'

'Sit down. There's no need to hurry away, is there? Have you a few moments to spare?'

'Not really, Mr. Cotes. Pearl's waiting for me downstairs. We go home together.'

'I see.' He looked disappointed. 'Well, in that case. . . .'

Richard Hindon walked in. He looked from one to the other.

'Won't keep you a minute, Richard.' Graham Cotes followed Carolyn to the door. 'Just a moment, Miss Lyle.'

Carolyn turned. Mr. Cotes looked at his watch. 'Could you—I wondered—are you busy tonight?'

'Well, I was going to wash my hair, but it can wait. Why?'

He was so hesitant, perhaps because of the presence of the other man, that she wished she could help him out. 'I wondered if—we could do what we did the other evening. You know, have a meal somewhere. . . .'

'Not a meal, Mr. Cotes. My grandmother will have it ready for me when I get in.'

'Afterwards, then? A show, or a film?' He looked at her, appeal in his eyes.

She turned on a bright smile. 'That would be nice.' They arranged a time and place to meet. 'Till later then, Mr. Cotes.' She looked past him into his room. 'Goodnight, Mr. Hindon.'

But Mr. Hindon did not answer. His look ran

through her and she felt as if she had been struck by lightning.

The film had been good and they had enjoyed it. Now they were sitting in a nearby restaurant drinking coffee and eating biscuits.

They had been discussing the film and laughing a lot and now they were quiet. She asked a question which had been on her mind the whole evening.

'What did Mr. Hindon say when I left you and went home?'

Graham, as he had asked her to call him, smiled and fiddled with his spoon. 'He said plenty.' He hesitated. 'Shall I tell you? All right, but you may not like it. He said—was I in my right mind in asking you out? He saw you, he said, behaving in an abandoned way on the beach last night with your boy-friend——'

'It's not true,' she cried.

'I'm sure it isn't, but I told him that if it was, then he had no right to be looking.' He laughed reminiscently. 'He nearly sent me flying across the room for that. He said you were a promiscuous little b—sorry, my dear, witch—a provocative, impudent little firebrand and not under any circumstances to be trusted.'

She unclenched her hands and put them up to her burning cheeks. If she had not already known what he thought of her, she certainly did now.

'I told him I knew very well what I was doing in going out with a girl as charming and innocent as you are.' He laughed again. 'He said, "Is she hell!" and nearly threw something at me. I also told him I was under no illusions and had my dreams firmly under control, and that the only reason you were going out with me was because, lonely old bachelor-type that I am, I had been unscrupulous and played on your sympathies and you were only going out with me out of pity. I also said that if he kept on trying to warn me off you, I could only conclude that he was jealous and wanted you himself.'

'Then what?' she whispered.

'He just stopped himself from punching me on the nose, made an uncomplimentary and rather rude remark about you and slammed the door between us.'

Her mouth was parched and her vocal organs seemed to have seized up. So it was even worse than she had thought. He really hated her. He had not relented and accepted her as she hoped he might.

'I—I didn't know Mr. Hindon could lose his temper like that,' she mumbled, making a feeble attempt at a joke to give herself a chance to normalise her feelings.

'My dear Carolyn, when that man gets angry, really angry, I'm warning you, stand clear or you might get hurt.'

She recalled the vicious tug on her hair the night she baby-sat at his sister's house and knew that Graham was speaking the truth.

'I'm sorry,' she said in a subdued tone, 'to have been the cause of a quarrel between you. Perhaps it would be better if I—if we——'

He looked disturbed. 'Carolyn, I'm not being deprived of a few precious hours in your company because of the disapproval of another man—one, moreover, who has no right either to approve or disapprove.'

She was appalled by the apparent depth of his feelings for her. 'But, Graham, is it wise——?'

'I told you, my dear,' he said gently, 'I can contain my dreams.'

She murmured, half to herself, seeking a solution to the problem, 'There's Pearl....' She recalled Pearl's reaction when she had told her on the bus of her date with Mr. Cotes. She had been shocked, then envious, then a little sad. 'He's a nice man,' she'd said, 'a very nice man.'

Graham seemed to be only half listening. 'What

about Pearl?' Then he was on to her train of thought and laughed. 'Are you trying to marry me off? Because if so, you can save your breath. While you're around, unattached and heartwhole, I'll never look at another woman.'

She looked at him, thinking he might be joking, but the seriousness of his eyes gave him away. He took her home. They sat in the car, still and silent. Carolyn half-turned towards him, waiting.

'My dear child,' he said, so quietly and so gently she could hardly hear him, 'there's no need for you to thank me in the usual fashion. I wouldn't dream of forcing myself on you.'

She saw his profile in the light of the street lamp. She wished that she wanted to kiss him, but there was nothing there. If she did, she knew, and he would know, that she would be doing it out of pity and for no other reason. Shyly, her hand reached out and touched his. He covered her hand with his free one.

'You're a wonderful girl,' he whispered, and she wanted to cry. She got out of the car and he drove away.

Next morning Keith White greeted her, 'Boss's orders—Miss Lyle not to be allowed on counter duty again until she's learnt the rules as well as she knows the alphabet and really knows what she's about. So it's menial tasks for you for the time being, Carolyn,' he teased her.

Carolyn had half expected it. Richard Hindon's standards were so high, she knew he would not readily overlook the mistakes she had made. Keith gave her clerical duties and she spent her time writing reserva-ton cards and overdue notices. She filled in catalogue cards, filed away magazines and pushed book-laden trolleys round the floor.

She was standing in the book store wondering what to do next when someone stood behind her and put an arm across her shoulders. Startled, she turned to see Graham Cotes beside her.

'Hallo, Carolyn. Why the surprise? Who did you think it was—the chief himself?'

She laughed at his ironic joke. 'Busy?' he asked.

'Haven't stopped all day.'

'Well, I've got a job for you.' He led her to the door, his arm still round her, and Carolyn noticed that Richard was down there again, talking to Miss Stagg. Why, she wondered miserably, did he visit the lending section so often these days? To spy on her, to catch her out again?

Graham lifted his free hand and pointed to the walls near the entrance, then indicated the notice board. He bent his head and whispered in her ear, trying not to disturb the readers, 'See those notices?' Out of the corner of her eye, Carolyn saw that Richard was watching them. 'They're nearly all out of date, so I want you to take them down and throw them away. Then I've got some new ones I want you to put in their place.'

She smiled and whispered back, 'D'you think I can manage such a difficult job?'

He squeezed her arm. 'I think so. I don't hold such a low opinion of your mental powers as does our boss over there.'

They both glanced at the man he was referring to and caught his cold stare. 'I,' said Graham, removing his arm, 'must be on my way, before I get turned to stone.'

'I'll do it soon,' she promised, and he left her.

There was a disturbance at the entrance doors and a young woman walked past the counter with a child beside her and another in a push-chair. She saw Carolyn and made straight for her. The little boy in the push-chair jumped up and down and thrust out his arms as stiff as iron bars. He stretched his fingers and shouted,

'Caroly! Caroly! *Basi want Caroly!*'

Carolyn stared, horrified at the noise he was making. The readers turned from their books, the staff looked up from their work, but Basi's mother did not stop until she was across the room and standing in front of her.

Hilary said, 'Carolyn, I'd like to ask you——' but the little boy began again. He struggled to free himself from the restraining strap across his middle, and made such a din that Carolyn stooped down, lifted him up and held him in her arms. Only then was he quiet.

Helen said, 'Naughty Basi. You'll annoy Uncle Rich. He's over there,' and she pointed.

Basi started again, 'Unker Rich, Unker Rich,' and jumped up and down with such energy that Carolyn could hardly hold him.

Richard was across the room in a few strides. Under the cover of insistent and endless 'Unker Riches' he hissed to Hilary, 'What the hell have you come here for?'

'Only to ask Carolyn about——'

'For God's sake keep that boy quiet. You'd better come up to my room. You too, Miss Lyle.' But Basi would not be put off. He 'Unker Riched' until his uncle turned and snatched him from Carolyn's arms.

'Now will you keep quiet, you little devil!' he muttered so that only the little group could hear.

In his room, he set the child down in the push-chair, but Basi struggled out and crawled under the desk. Helen tried to pull him out by the legs, but Basi won. He turned and regarded them like a dog at the door of his kennel.

Roseanna Harvey came in and stopped in her tracks. 'Oh, what a lovely little boy,' she cooed affectedly, and put out her arms to him. But Basi scrambled up and hid his face in Carolyn's legs.

Hilary nodded and smiled at her brother's secretary

117

and Richard said, 'Did you want something, Mrs. Harvey?'

'Only to see if you wanted rescuing,' she twittered sympathetically.

'I—er—I think I can look after myself, Roseanna,' he answered with a smile. 'If not, I shall call for help.'

'Ugh,' Carolyn thought, and felt sick inside.

He watched his secretary withdraw herself inch by inch and turned to his sister. 'Whatever you want to say, say it and go. Then perhaps we can get back to normal.'

'Sorry, Richard. I'm always putting my foot in it where you're concerned, aren't I?' From her tone, she seemed to be genuinely sorry, and Carolyn warmed to her. How Hilary remained so good-tempered with her brother, she couldn't understand.

'It's about baby-sitting,' Hilary said, watching Helen following Basi round the room and taking away from him everything he picked up. 'Tomorrow. Is the notice too short? Some friends are calling for me after lunch and taking me to town.'

Richard sat at his desk and started working.

'Then we're wining and dining and going to a show. If you can come in the evening, my neighbour will give the children their tea.'

'But I could do that,' Carolyn offered. 'It's my Saturday afternoon off, so I won't be working then. In fact, if you like, I'll come straight after lunch, before you leave.'

Hilary's eyes shone. 'Would you really? My dear, that's marvellous. Richard's going out,' the man in question did not stir, 'so the house would be empty otherwise.'

They arranged a time, then Hilary said, 'I'm giving a party next week. I'd love you to come and bring your fabulous boy-friend.'

'Which one?' came a dry voice from the desk.

Hilary looked puzzled and Carolyn said hastily, 'I'm sure Shane would love to come. Thank you very much.'

'Well, I'll be off,' said Hilary, looking at her brother's bent head. He rose, swept Basi away from the large books he was conscientiously sliding off the shelf and on to the floor, and dumped him in the pushchair.

'Tidy those up, Miss Lyle, then get back to your work, fast. I'll see my sister out the back way.'

Carolyn caught Hilary's look of sympathy as she bent down, suddenly weary, to do his bidding. The room was quiet when they had gone and she sagged, still crouching, against Richard's chair. His jacket was hanging across the back of it and she rubbed her cheek slowly up and down the sleeve. Then she finished putting the books away and went back to work.

Carolyn hung her jacket in the hall cupboard and joined Hilary in the kitchen. 'The children have their tea about five,' Hilary told her. 'Richard's out and he'll have his meal out, too. So you can forget about him.'

When Hilary had gone, Carolyn sat in the garden while the children played on the swing and scrambled over the climbing frame. The warm sunshine relaxed her and as she breathed in the flower scents, she felt the tensions which had been building up over the past weeks slide off and melt away like snow in a thaw.

Every time her thoughts reached out, like a wayward child, towards the man she had the misfortune to love, she hauled them back and forced herself to think of something else. But it was difficult to stop them straining in his direction, sitting as she was under the windows of the room he lived in.

The children were getting restive and went indoors. Carolyn followed. They had gone upstairs and their uncle's door was open. She found Basi wandering round the room, picking up his uncle's possessions and throwing them on the floor.

'Stop it, Basi,' Carolyn said, rescuing them. 'Uncle Rich won't like it.'

'Oh,' said Helen, 'Uncle Rich won't be back for ages and ages. He never is on Saturdays.'

Basi made a sudden lunge and Carolyn watched with horror as he fastened his hands on to the base of a holder packed with records.

She dived to save them and sent flying a chess board set out with chessmen. She gasped and Helen tutted. 'Uncle Rich will be very angry. He was when I did it once. He nearly smacked my bottom.'

Carolyn went on her knees to retrieve the chess pieces and Helen helped. 'I know,' said Helen, 'let's put them back on the board and hope he doesn't notice.'

'Hope he doesn't notice what?' His footsteps must have been as light as a ghost's and he stood in the doorway frowning. 'What's going on in here? This is forbidden territory.' His eyes swung to Carolyn, still on her knees. 'And what the devil are you doing down there?'

Helen backed away from him and spread her hands behind her. 'I didn't do it, Uncle Rich. Don't smack me.'

Carolyn stayed where she was, clutching the white queen in her hand as if it were some magic talisman which would protect her from Richard's wrath.

'Didn't do what? Miss Lyle, can you explain?'

But Miss Lyle couldn't. The words wouldn't come.

'Caroly did it,' sang Basi, 'Caroly did it.'

'And what precisely did "Caroly" do?' His eyes became speculative as they moved from her to the chess board leaning drunkenly against the legs of a chair. He saw the scattered chessmen. 'Ah, now I get it.' He advanced towards her, hands thrust into pockets. 'So it's you I have to spank, is it, Miss Lyle?'

'Of *course* not, Mr. Hindon.' In her confusion, she

became indignant. She stood up and faced him. 'It was that or your records.'

'Oh, I see. So—no spank?'

She shook her head emphatically. 'No spank.'

And he, with a smile, imitated the shake of her head and moved away. 'Pity,' he sighed. He sat in a fireside chair, pulled the coffee table towards him and set out the chess pieces on the board. He rubbed his chin. 'That's it, I think.'

'You remember where they all went?'

He looked up into Carolyn's astonished face. 'Of course I do. All good chess players remember the positions of the pieces.'

'But suppose a board's knocked over in the middle of a game?'

'Even then. The players will just put them back.' He looked at the board. 'But this isn't a game—it's a chess problem. A big difference—more creative and, to me, more satisfying, because at the end of it you have, as it were, created a work of art. And it's solitary,' he glanced up at her, 'which I like. It suits my nature.'

She turned away, remembering—in fact, she couldn't forget—the bleakness in his face that evening on the sea front. So he liked his loneliness, did he?

'Why did you come back early today, Uncle Rich?' Helen asked. 'You usually stay out all night.'

He threw back his head and laughed. 'My word, you'll give Miss Lyle the wrong impression if you tell her that! But I don't really, Helen. I come back long after you're in bed. I just—changed my mind today.'

Carolyn answered, so that only he could hear, 'I can tell you why—because he doesn't trust me to look after you without supervision.'

Richard raised an eyebrow, smiled maddeningly and gave his attention to the chess board.

Basi made a dive for his uncle's legs and Carolyn watched apprehensively as the boy clambered on to his lap. Richard was immediately on the defensive. Basi must have felt the sudden tensing of his uncle's body because he grabbed at the first thing he could find which would act as an anchor. His fingers closed on Richard's tie. Richard's hand came up and tried to tug the boy's hand away. But Basi clung.

'Leave go, you little devil,' his uncle growled. 'And get down.'

Ruthlessly he prised off the clutching fingers and dumped the boy on the floor. Basi opened his mouth and yelled.

Carolyn, smouldering with anger, scooped him on to her lap and held his sobbing body. 'How could you?' she cried. 'How could you treat him like that?' her voice rose. 'Can't you see he loves you? Are you deaf and blind to everyone else's feelings? Must you reject *everybody*, even those who—who love you?'

Richard stared at her, uncomprehending, like someone trying to interpret a foreign tongue. There was a long silence and Carolyn began to count the cost of her impetuous outburst.

Richard pushed back his chair, said 'Basi?' and stretched out his hands towards the child. Basi, silent now, scrambled eagerly off Carolyn's lap and on to his uncle's. Perfectly content, he snuggled down in his uncle's arms.

'Satisfied?' Richard mouthed over the boy's head. Carolyn smiled, nodded and turned aside.

'I'm hungry,' Helen said. 'When's tea?'

Carolyn looked at her watch. 'We'll get it now, if you like.'

'Can you cook, Miss Lyle?' She saw his taunting grin and nodded, wondering what was coming next.

'My, my,' he drawled, 'beauty, brains *and* domesticity, plus an overlarge dose of maternal instinct into the bargain. Some man's going to find you useful one day.' Still the taunting grin. 'Note the omission of the word "lucky" in front of "man".' He paused, dwelling on her angry eyes. 'That was intentional.'

She slammed the door and stalked into the kitchen. With Helen's willing help she prepared the tea, then wondered what to do about Richard. There was nothing for it—she would have to ask him if he wanted any food, although after his last remark, she felt like letting him go hungry.

She tapped on his door and went in. Basi was still curled up on his lap and appeared to be asleep. Carolyn noted that he looked a little pale.

'Will you be eating out, Mr. Hindon?' she asked, her tone sharp.

He leaned back in his chair and took his time in answering.

'I wasn't thinking of doing so. But judging by the lack of invitation in your voice, it would seem that you want me to.'

She was disconcerted by his directness. 'Well, I suppose I could cook you something. . . .'

'Such as?'

'Oh, an omelette, a cheese omelete, perhaps.'

He rested his head on the chair back and surveyed her. 'Now a cheese omelette cooked by the chairman's niece, that should taste delectable. Yes, please.'

She walked across the room and stood in front of him. 'Basi?' she said. 'Come along, darling. Tea's ready.'

He stirred and his eyes seemed heavy. He resisted her outstretched hand and his uncle looked down at him. 'Perhaps he's too comfortable,' he said.

But Carolyn persisted. Again the boy rejected her hand. He clutched his middle. ''Urt,' he said.

Richard looked up at her, worried. 'D'you think he's putting it on? We'll ask my intelligent niece. Helen,' he called. She came in. 'Basi says he's got a pain.'

She frowned. 'He might have. I had one the other day. Perhaps he's caught it. Or perhaps he's hungry. Come *on*, Basi. Have your tea.' She tugged him off Richard's lap and this time he didn't resist. But he dragged his feet as she led him downstairs.

He ate his tea with reasonable appetite so Carolyn stopped worrying about him. All the same she wished his mother was not miles away in London. She cooked Richard's omelette and carried it up to him on a tray. He took it from her absently, his mind now being fully on the chess problem he was composing, and his brief 'Thanks' dismissed her.

She washed up and got Basi to bed. She put him into his cot and he settled down immediately. Then it was Helen's turn. Carolyn undid the short, fair plaits and combed them.

'What do you do with your plaits when you go to bed?' Helen asked, touching them.

A voice from the landing said, 'Now that's what I'd like to know.'

Carolyn forced herself not to look round. 'Oh, sometimes I leave them as they are and comb them in the morning and sometimes I undo them and tie my hair back with a ribbon.'

'I wish my hair was that colour,' Helen murmured. 'It must look lovely all fluffed out.'

There was a sound which could have been a murmur of agreement from behind her and Carolyn glanced round, but Richard had gone.

Later, she went downstairs looking forward to a quiet evening alone, but Richard seemed to have other ideas. He was in the lounge reading. She recovered quickly from her surprise and sat opposite him. She tried to read, too, but she could not concentrate.

To break the heavy silence, she said, 'Your sister's children are very good about going to bed.'

He lowered his book and said dryly, 'They have to be. They've been well disciplined. My sister's a night bird. She needs her husband back to keep her in—and in order.'

'Well, I'm sorry for her. With her husband away, she must be very lonely.'

This really roused him. '*Sorry* for her? *Lonely?* My dear girl, don't waste your pity. My sister's been cosseted since birth, first by our parents, then in her late teens she married a man old enough to be her father, and he took over the cosseting. He worships her—there's no other word for it. He can't do enough for her. The irony of it is that she looks upon him as a benign provider of the luxuries of life, nothing else. And the poor fool can't see it. He thinks she's perfect. Watching their marriage at close quarters has put me off marriage for life.'

She felt tears gathering behind her eyes and by sheer self-control kept them there. When she was able to talk she said,

'How could you have allowed such bitterness to curdle your view of your sister to such an extent? My uncle was so fond of his sister—my mother—that when she died and my father left me alone, he devoted part of his life and a large portion of his income to giving his sister's child—me—everything he knew his sister would have wanted me to have if she'd lived.'

He didn't speak for a long time. Then he said softly and with absolute sincerity, 'Your mother must have been an angel.'

She fought for control again, then said, with a sincerity which equalled his own, 'What a pity I don't take after her.'

'Now who's being bitter?'

'I'm not being bitter. I'm just stating the truth.'

Their eyes met for a moment, then, because the lump was in her throat again, she picked up her book and hid behind its pages.

There was a shout from the landing. 'Carolyn, Basi's crying. I think he's got a pain.'

Carolyn flung down her book and was up the stairs almost before Helen had finished calling. The boy's cries were deafening as she opened his door and lifted him over the side of the cot. She walked up and down the room in the semi-darkness—the only light came from the landing—she talked to him, tried to soothe him and asked him what was wrong. He couldn't tell her.

Richard held out a cup of water. 'Any good?'

She took it, sat down with Basi on her knee and offered him the water. He turned his head away, but he stopped crying and lay still.

She whispered to Richard, 'Is he asleep?'

Richard came close and his forehead brushed against Carolyn's hair as he bent over the boy. He nodded. She lifted Basi into the cot, covered him and crept out of the room. When she returned to the lounge, she found she was alone.

CHAPTER SEVEN

THE evening passed slowly. She could not concentrate on her book, so she switched on the television, but she didn't see a thing, so she turned it off. Then she started thinking and her thoughts were painful, but she could not switch those off. She was tired now and began to long for Hilary's return.

She heard footsteps in the hall and tensed. She didn't want company and most of all she didn't want Richard. He opened the door and looked at her, then at his watch.

'Good God, twelve-thirty, already Sunday morning. The long, long vigil goes on.' He closed the door and stood in front of her. His jacket was off, his tie had been removed and there was a certain strain—it could have been fatigue—round his eyes which was not usually there. 'What does my sister think she's playing at? You've had her kids the whole afternoon, the whole evening—and now it looks like the whole night. Er—just out of interest, Miss Lyle, how much is my sister paying you? Because this little lot's going to cost her a packet.'

She did not answer at first, then, avoiding his eyes, she muttered, 'We discussed terms and we were both satisfied.'

'In other words, mind my own business.' He folded his arms. 'I suppose it's so much, you're ashamed to tell me.'

This brought her to life and she snapped, 'If you insist on knowing something that isn't your concern, I'm doing it for nothing.'

'You're *what*? You must be crazy, woman.' Then his surprise evaporated and his eyes became calculating. He said, nastily, 'You wouldn't be doing it to impress me, would you, Miss Lyle?'

She faced him angrily. 'Don't be ridiculous! You wouldn't have known, would you, if you hadn't provoked me into answering?'

The telephone rang. 'This,' said Richard, 'sounds ominous. Unless it's your grandmother getting worried about you?'

'It couldn't be. She's away for the weekend. She's staying with her sister.' She followed him into the hall.

Richard said, 'Who's that? Hilary? Look here, what do you——?' He glanced at Carolyn. 'Yes, of course she's still here. But she's nearly asleep on her feet—what?'

He turned and thrust the receiver into Carolyn's hand. 'She insists on talking to you. You'll have to listen carefully. I think she's half tight.'

'Hilary?' Carolyn said.

'My dear, I'm so sorry about this, but it really is impossible for me to get back tonight. You'll have to get Richard to take you home again. I'm still in London. We've been to a night club,' her words were slurring slightly, 'and we've decided to make a night of it and put up at this hotel. I'll be back about midmorning, but Richard will have to cope with the kids till then. You go home, my dear.'

Richard hissed into Carolyn's ear, 'Tell her about the boy.'

Carolyn shook her head. Richard's fingers closed over hers and he tried to wrench the receiver away. 'I will, then.'

She saw he was in earnest and said, 'Hilary, Basi's not well. He keeps getting a pain——'

'Oh dear, has he caught it from Helen? I thought he might.'

Richard was standing beside her and could hear his sister's voice clearly. He shook his head, disgusted. 'And she still went out,' he said.

Hilary went on, 'Well, it can't be helped, Richard'll have to cope, if necessary.'

'But, Hilary——'

'Carolyn dear, I've just had a thought—you couldn't stay the night, could you, just in case Basi gets worse?' Carolyn heard a swift incredulous intake of breath beside her. 'You could have my bed and help yourself to all my things—what about your gran? Would she worry?'

'Well, no, she's away, but——'

'My dear, if it's Richard you're worrying about, there's no need to be afraid of staying in the house with him. He's such a crusty old bachelor that if a woman stood in front of him and pleaded with him to kiss her, he wouldn't even know how to start!' She laughed uproariously into Carolyn's ear. 'So you stay, my dear. I think that's the answer, in which case I'll see you in the morning. Just wear my nightie and get a clean towel and so on. I must go. Thanks a lot, dear. Love to my brother. 'Bye.'

Carolyn put the phone down and did not dare to turn her head.

'It's out of the question,' Richard snapped. 'I'm taking you home.'

There was a wail from upstairs. 'It's Basi,' Carolyn said. 'The phone must have disturbed him.' She raced up the stairs and went into Basi's room. He was doubled up with pain and she picked him up and held him close. He whimpered for a while, then, when he was quiet, she lowered him into the cot and tiptoed out.

'I can't understand it,' she whispered to Richard on the landing. 'It might be serious. Could even be appendicitis.' She looked at him appealingly. 'I'll have to stay, Mr. Hindon.'

She returned to the lounge for her handbag and he followed her.

'Well, it's your decision. You heard what my sister

129

said.' His smile taunted her. 'She asserts, with the mindless arrogance of sisters, that I'm desexed. I'm entirely neuter. So you're quite safe with me, aren't you?' He walked towards her. 'Unless you'd care to put theory to the test? I'm warning you, though, the result might prove to be the exact opposite of her contention.'

As he stood in front of her, hands on hips, legs slightly apart, he looked so challenging and so dangerously attractive that it took an enormous effort of will on her part to resist his magnetism.

She made for the door. 'I'm—I'm going up. If you'll just tell me which is your sister's room....'

On the landing he pointed. 'That one.' He grinned sardonically. 'I hope you appreciate her taste in night attire and that you enjoy wearing it.' He eyed her up and down. 'You may not be quite so—er—shall we say, voluptuous as she is, but you're none the less shapely, so it should fit well enough. Goodnight.' He turned and left her.

She looked round the bedroom, with its soft lights and lavish furnishings, its fabulously soft golden eiderdown and floor-length curtains to match. Everywhere there were the initials 'H.R.', on the pillow cases, dressing-table mats, handkerchiefs and towels. Carolyn took the black nightdress from its elaborate case and gasped at its gossamer-like transparency. No wonder Hilary's brother had commented on it!

She found a clean towel in the airing cupboard, washed quickly and closed the bedroom door. She undid her plaits and combed her waist-length hair until it sparked and spread in a pale gold cascade around her. She tied it loosely behind her neck and slipped into the nightdress.

For a long time sleep would not come. She could not relax, nor could she stop thinking, and her thoughts were all of the man across the landing. At last she drifted into a dream and was deeply asleep when the touch of a hand disturbed her.

She fought back to consciousness and realised that the light was on and someone was shaking her and calling her name. 'Carolyn, it's Basi.' Richard was bending over her. 'He's crying. I think he's ill. Could you come?'

She could hear Basi's cries and sat up, forgetting about the flimsiness of the nightdress she was wearing. Still not fully awake, she looked up at Richard, and remembered. Hastily she pulled the blankets round her. 'Is there a dressing-gown I could wear?'

He smiled. 'You could wear my sister's—it's hanging on the door—but it's just as inadequate as the thing you're wearing. Here,' he took off his own dressing-gown and put it on the bed. 'Wear this. I'll find a coat.'

He went out and she hugged Richard's large dressing-gown round her, holding it up to avoid tripping over the hem. She ran into Basi's room, but she was too late. He was sitting up, pale and miserable and in a shocking mess. He had been sick and she could see at a glance that the cot would have to be stripped of its coverings and entirely re-made. She lifted him out and handed him over to Richard, who produced some clean pyjamas and proceeded to wash and change him.

Carolyn stripped the cot, and found clean sheets and blankets in cupboards and drawers. Then, while Richard watched, she took up the shaken little boy and rocked him gently in her arms. He turned towards her and buried his face in the depths of her hair which was hanging loose and untied around her.

'Basi love Caroly,' he muttered, half-asleep. 'Basi love Unker Rich.'

At last Carolyn felt him relax into sleep, a deep true sleep, and for the last time that night she put him back into his cot.

On the landing, in the semi-darkness, Richard

caught her arm. His hands came up and imprisoned her face and he whispered, 'Thank you, Carolyn, for looking after my nephew so devotedly and so patiently. You've—almost—restored my faith in women.'

She looked up into his face, so near to hers.

'Goodnight, Carolyn,' he whispered.

'Goodnight, Mr.——' A finger pressed her lips and she heard a decisive 'no'. 'Goodnight, Richard,' she whispered back.

Then he moved and she felt him reach out and take up two great handfuls of her hair. He lowered his head and buried his face in them. Her legs became unsteady. Another minute and she would have had to cling to him for support.

He dropped her hair, turned her round and, with his hands on her shoulders, walked her to her bedroom door. He pushed her in, closed the door and went away.

It was Monday morning. Carolyn stirred sleepily in her bed, reluctant to face the day. She thought about her conversation with Hilary on the phone the previous evening. She had apologised profusely—Carolyn was getting used to that now—and told her that Basi was back to normal.

'Only too much so,' she said, ruefully. 'I hear Richard took you home after breakfast. He's been like a bear all day. I don't know what's the matter with him. Don't forget my party on Wednesday, Carolyn. And make sure you bring your Shane, won't you?'

'Anyone would think,' Carolyn had laughed, 'that you had designs on him!'

'What, me—take away your boy-friend? My dear, I wouldn't dream of such a thing.' Her laughter had filled the receiver.

Before leaving for work, Carolyn tidied the house for her grandmother's return. She put the book she had borrowed from Richard into her hold-all. That afternoon, after work, she would return it to him.

As she pushed through the library entrance doors, she sensed a tension in the members of staff already there, and this was confirmed when Graham came down the strairs and made straight for her.

He put his hand on her shoulder. 'Steer clear of the boss today, Carolyn. You especially. He's in a foul mood and you're his *bête noire*, so he'll pour out his wrath on you if you give him half a chance.' He looked round. 'Did you take—great heavens, Carolyn, you haven't taken down those notices! For goodness' sake, do it now before he spots it.'

But it was too late. Richard Hindon was there, his face taut, his mouth a thin tight line, watching them. 'Miss Lyle,' he rapped out, 'why have those out-of-date notices not been removed? Can you not even do a simple job like that without someone to prop you up and give you special tuition?'

'But, Mr. Hindon,' Carolyn protested, 'I only forgot them because your sister——'

He was not listening. 'I will not have out-of-date notices sprawling over the walls of my library. There are enough ancient monuments cluttering up the place, thanks to the machinations of your uncle, without adding to them. And don't bring my sister into it. She's not responsible for your negligence.'

When he had gone, Graham pressed her arm. 'I did warn you, didn't I? When you've finished, come up to my room for the new notices. But come in an armoured car, in case the boss is with me!'

The boss was not with him. She put the new notices round the walls in what she considered to be a more attractive arrangement. Keith complimented her on her artistic leanings, but it didn't please the chief librarian. He told her curtly to take them all down and put them up in order of date and importance, giving more prominence to the local societies than to 'outsiders', as he put it.

She told him she disagreed and that her arrangement would draw reasonable attention to all of them, without the favouritism he seemed to be preaching.

'I didn't ask for your opinion,' he said shortly, adding sarcastically, 'I think I am in a better position to judge local needs than you are, Miss Lyle, despite your close connection with officialdom.'

So she had taken them all down and put them up again in the order which he had dictated. She pushed the drawing pins home with such force that she narrowly missed pinning her thumbs to the wall.

Keith came towards her with a pile of book jackets. 'These are new arrivals. Would you take down all those fixed to that "new editions" board over there and put these in their place? Another thing—like to tackle a book display?' She looked puzzled and he explained, 'Now and then we want to bring to the notice of the public a certain subject of, say, current political or cultural interest. One of us is given the job of choosing the subject and selecting books related to it from the shelves and displaying them in a prominent place in the library. We make our own posters to go with them—ever done any lettering? No? Well, I'll have to teach you. You never know, you may discover you've got a flair for it—artistic ability and all that. But first I'll have to get permission from the chief for you to do it, since you haven't been here long. Although personally I think you're quite capable of tackling it.'

She thanked him for those few kind words and he tweaked one of her plaits as he walked away.

That evening, she decided to brave the chief librarian's bad temper and ask his secretary if he was free. He was, and looked up irritably when she went in. She held out his book. He took it without a word.

'I enjoyed reading it, Mr. Hindon. I've learnt a lot from it.'

He nodded and seemed to be waiting impatiently for her to go. She did not go, however. She asked him, 'Did Mr. White mention to you about——'

'About your tackling a book display? Yes. I turned the idea down.'

'Why, Mr. Hindon? He thought I was capable of doing it.'

'I'm sorry, but I didn't agree.'

'But it's something I'd love to do,' she cried.

He insisted quietly, 'I said "no", Miss Lyle.'

She waited for a moment, then asked, 'Can I go back on counter duty soon, Mr. Hindon? I enjoyed it the short time I did it.'

'When I consider you're ready for it, Miss Lyle.'

She protested, near to tears now and losing her caution, 'You're not giving me a fair chance. I can't do anything right for you. No matter how hard I try, it's never enough. Even things I enjoy doing you won't let me do.' Then the tears did come, she couldn't hold them back. 'You're conducting a vendetta against me, because of who I am. You're so prejudiced where I'm concerned that according to you I've only got faults, not virtues. It's not right that someone in your position should be so biased against a member of his staff.'

'*That will do, Miss Lyle!*' His biting tone brought back her reason. He leaned back in his chair. 'Getting emotional and weeping won't help you. If you would just try to be rational and consider the facts, you will realise that you're introducing the personal element. I'm not. You may be a University graduate in the big outside world, but here in this library you're a junior —a very junior—assistant. You've got a lot—a hell of a lot—to learn. It's not in your interests nor the interests of the library service, to let you do anything just because you "enjoy" doing it, when, because of lack of experience, you are simply not capable of doing it properly.' He watched her take out her handkerchief and dry her eyes. 'So you can stop questioning my

135

impartiality and fairness, and you can withdraw your preposterous charges of vendettas and prejudice, and apologise.'

She did, haltingly and almost inaudibly.

'And remember something else, Miss Lyle.' He looked at her coldly. 'I'm in charge here. You, like all the others, take your orders from me, regardless of whether or not you approve of them, and regardless of your privileged background.' He looked down at his work. 'Thank you for returning my book.'

Alone on the bus, on the way home, she cried a little for the man who, in a moment of weakness, on the landing in the dark, had buried his face in her hair.

Carolyn phoned Shane to tell him about Hilary's party. Her uncle answered, and asked how she was getting on.

'Very well,' she told him, crossing her fingers firmly.

'I'm calling in again soon, dear—just to check up on things. I like to keep my eye on Mr. Librarian Hindon. You never know what he's up to otherwise. Here's Shane now.'

'Hallo, sweetie,' said Shane, and he whispered, probably because his stepfather was still within earshot, 'How's the big bad boss?'

'I—he—well, he....' Carolyn stumbled over her answer.

'All right, sweet, I get it. Say no more. As big and bad as ever. It's obvious you need a little comfort, and I'm the one to give you that, aren't I?'

She laughed. 'Are you? I wouldn't know. You remember I told you about Hilary? Well, she's having a party on Wednesday and by special request I'm to take you. I think she's taken a fancy to you!'

'Has she now? I'm most flattered. What's her husband doing about these "fancies" of hers?'

'He's away for a few months.'

'Now things are really getting interesting.'

'Look, Shane, if I take you you must promise to behave. She's Richard Hindon's sister, remember, and things are bad enough between us without you introducing complications.'

'All right, I'll try to be a good boy. I'll pick you up—when?'

They arranged a time and rang off.

For the party, Carolyn wore a yellow sleeveless dress. One of her plaits she twisted into a coronet about her head, the other she pulled to the front and allowed to hang loose. The result was both innocent and worldly and consequently intriguing.

She stood beside Shane in Hilary's lounge, drinking sherry and listening to the chatter around her. Hilary's eyes were turned up to Shane's, openly admiring him. He was lapping it up, and Carolyn wished he would be a little more discreet in his response to Hilary's provocation. Every time the door opened, she looked round anxiously in case Richard came in.

But as time went on, and he did not appear, she began to wonder if he would come at all. Hilary moved to her side. 'There's one person who won't flatter us with his presence, Carolyn. Guess who? My beloved brother. He hates parties, but more particularly he can't stand my friends.' She laughed as she moved away. 'He'll probably go out, and good riddance to him.'

Carolyn sat on the couch, weary with disappointment.

She stared through the french windows and wished she could escape into the sunlit garden without attracting attention. She decided to try. As she was rising from the couch a hand fastened on to her arm and pulled her back.

'Where are you going to, my pretty maid?' The voice belonged to a young man wearing a flowered shirt and pink trousers. She wondered how he came to be rated as one of Hilary's 'friends', since he was more in her own age group than Hilary's.

'Wherever it is,' he went on, his eyes busy all over her, 'can I come?'

'I've changed my mind,' Carolyn said, looking round for Shane. But he was preoccupied with a girl in a flowing ankle-length dress and an Elizabethan-type ruffle round her neck.

The young man next to Carolyn said, 'That's Jane you're looking at. She's an artist, like me. I don't know who her new boy-friend is.'

Carolyn laughed. 'That's Shane, *my* boy-friend.'

A long-fingered hand flew delicately to his forehead. 'My foot,' he lifted it up, 'always goes in it, right in it.' He examined Carolyn again, as though he were sizing her up for a portrait. 'You've got something, definitely something I should like to capture. On canvas, of course, on canvas.' He rolled back, weak with laughter.

'Carolyn,' Hilary drifted up to her, 'I think your Shane's marvellous, absolutely marvellous! Jonathan, my dear,' her hands came out to Carolyn's companion, 'how long have you been here, darling?'

'Oh, years,' he said. 'I've found myself an angel.' Hilary laughed and moved away. 'That hair,' Jonathan went on, shifting along the couch until he was pressing against Carolyn's side, 'that glorious hair.' He picked up the loose-hanging plait and put it to his cheek, then against his lips.

His other arm crept round her waist, and because Carolyn was already at the extreme end of the couch, she could not move away.

'Darling,' he said, 'undo it for Jonathan. The artist in me cries out to see it. It must look quite magnificent combed out and hanging free.'

'It does,' came a dry, sardonic voice in front of them, 'especially at three o'clock in the morning.'

Carolyn struggled free of Jonathan's hold and glared at the speaker, who was leaning nonchalantly against the wall, glass in hand, watching them. He looked as though he had been there a long time.

Even Jonathan seemed momentarily to lose his poise as the implication behind the words came through. He moved away quickly.

'Oh, God,' he said, waggling his foot, 'it's gone in it again.' He looked at Richard. 'Is she your woman, or something?' He eased himself upright, looked shiftily at Richard, waved his hand to indicate that his seat was free and wandered off.

Richard took Jonathan's place. 'Sorry to have broken up the new friendship, so touchingly intimate it was, too.'

She bristled at his cynicism and turned on him. Now that he was there, she had forgotten completely the time she had spent longing for him to come. 'I thought you never came to your sister's parties. I thought you didn't like her friends.'

'The answer to both those statements is the same. I don't, usually. This time I have, but only to observe, not to join in the fun.' He tossed his drink down his throat and put the glass on a tray. 'You have an attentive boy-friend.' His nod indicated Shane, who was obviously getting more than friendly with Jane. 'Never mind, you didn't waste much time in filling his place, did you?'

His sarcasm was goading her so much that she clenched her fists and said, 'I wish you would go away. I wish you would leave me alone.'

He lifted himself slowly from the couch and went out.

The party grew noisier, the laughter more brittle, the atmosphere more intimate. Someone had brought in the food and someone had set the record player going. Carolyn sat beside Shane wondering how she could get away. She stood up and he didn't even notice. Hilary sat down beside him.

Carolyn edged to the door and closed it behind her, shutting in the shrieks of laughter and the drum-beat of the music. She went up to the bathroom to tidy herself. When she came out, Richard was on the land-

139

ing, staring down into the hall. She followed his eyes. Standing out of sight in a small recess were two figures locked in a passionate embrace—Hilary and Shane.

At last they moved apart and walked, hand in hand, along the hall, out of the kitchen door and into the garden.

Richard Hindon turned on her. 'Can't you keep your boy-friend under control? Are you so mean with your favours that he has to turn to a married woman—my sister—for the gratification of his desires?'

Carolyn faced him, refusing to be frightened by the latent violence which was implicit in his whole bearing. Her anger equalled his as she choked out, 'At least he has desires. His emotional temperature isn't minus zero like yours. At least he's human, he's not solid ice like you.'

'Echoes of my sister,' he snarled. 'You challenge me like that, *my pretty maid*, and you get exactly what you're asking for.'

He seized her bare arms and pulled her into his room. He kicked the door shut and threw her backwards against it. His mouth bore down on hers and she was engulfed by a kiss that was pitiless and brutal and acknowledged no restrictions. It aroused in her such a tumult of feeling that she was terrified by its magnitude. She fought to get away from him, but he tightened his hold and would not let her go until he was ready to do so.

It was not until he had put her out of the door and slammed it shut that she saw on her arms the pinpoints of blood which had been inflicted by his fingernails. She put her hands over her face. She was shaking uncontrollably. Graham's warning words drifted back into her mind—'When that man gets angry, stand clear or you might get hurt.' Well, she had made him angry, really angry, and she had taken the consequences.

Someone moved in the hall. A voice said, 'Who's up

there? Is that the girl they call Carolyn?'

She turned wildly—which room should she run to? Jonathan started up the stairs. Carolyn hurtled into the bathroom and locked the door.

'Hey,' the door handle rattled. 'Is that Carolyn? Come on, darling, I won't hurt you.'

Another door opened and a voice drawled, 'Sorry, old chap, this floor's out of bounds.'

'Then what's that redhead doing up here?'

'She—er—half belongs here. She's not for sale. Sorry.'

There came a long-drawn-out 'Oh—oh, I get it. All right, mate, I wouldn't dream of poaching. Some men have all the luck!'

Footsteps went down the stairs and there was a tap at the door. 'It's all right, Miss Lyle,' Richard said, 'you can come out now.'

She opened the door and tried to push past him, but his hand detained her. 'Where are you going?'

She jerked her arm away and went into Hilary's bedroom. 'Home.' She took up her coat and struggled into it.

'With your boy-friend?'

'No.'

'You know the last bus has gone?'

'I don't care. I'll walk.'

'I'll get my car out and take you.'

'I wouldn't go in your car,' she hissed, 'even if I had a hundred-mile trek in front of me!'

She ran down the stairs and out of the front door, but Richard was close behind. She started walking and when a car drew up beside her she walked faster.

'Get in!' Richard snapped.

She ignored him.

'I'll get you into this car somehow even if I'm arrested by a policeman for abduction.' She stopped. 'Now, get in.'

She got in and sat sullenly silent for the whole journey. When he drew up outside her house, he put his hand over hers and said softly, 'Goodnight, Carolyn.'

She didn't answer. She flung open the door and raced up the garden path. She couldn't have answered even if she had wanted to, because if she had, he would have known that she was crying.

Shane phoned first thing next morning. 'What happened to you last night? Big Bad Hindon gave me some tale about a headache. He said he'd taken you home.'

She told him it was true, Mr. Hindon had given her a lift.

'And another thing—that Jonathan chap put it round that you were Hindon's woman. His sister laughed her head off, but——'

'Of course it's not true, Shane. Jonathan followed me upstairs and Mr. Hindon put him off my scent. Anyway,' she took refuge in attack, 'you can't talk, Shane. I said "hands off Hilary", remember? We saw the two of you in the hall. . . .'

'My dear innocent little girl, when a woman practically asks a man. . . .'

'All right, I'll forgive you, but I doubt if her brother will.'

'Anyway, I took Jane home. You know, that nice little artistic type.'

'Then I did you a good turn, didn't I, in going home early!'

They laughed and rang off.

As Carolyn climbed the steps to the library entrance a little later, she wondered how much longer she could go on working there. Her relationship with Richard Hindon was becoming intolerable. Her love for him deepened every time she saw him and his dislike of her was apparently intensifying at the same frightening rate.

She had a headache. She looked round for Richard, dreading their first meeting, but she relaxed a little when she saw he was not there.

Shelf-tidying was her first task each morning and she worked her way round her section more slowly than usual. She knew why she was tired. She had lain awake for most of the night thinking about Richard.

The books on the top shelf badly needed rearranging and she lifted the step-stool into place—the ladder was already in use—and opened it out.

Keith called, 'I shouldn't use that, Carolyn. It's unstable. Wait until the ladder's free.'

But she climbed on to it impatiently. She tidied the books in front of her, then, instead of getting off the stool and moving it, she stretched her arm to reach the books just along the row.

She heard Richard say, 'Where's Miss Lyle? I want to see her.'

The shock of hearing his voice made her careless and she reached out too far. The stool rocked under her and she plunged sideways, her body hitting the floor with a sickening thump. Her head made heavy contact with the woodblock flooring and she lay still, stunned and winded.

She heard Richard catch his breath and say, 'Oh God, Carolyn!' Swiftly he came to her side, and she tried to reassure him with a smile, but it was too much of an effort. Others gathered round and Richard said, 'I'm going to lift you, Miss Lyle, and take you upstairs to my room.'

He carried her with a tenderness she never dreamed he possessed. He looked into her face and whispered, 'Am I hurting you, Carolyn?' When he bent his head to listen to her murmured 'No,' she caught the tang of his after-shave lotion.

He set her down gently in the visitors' armchair, drew another chair close and lifted her legs so that her feet rested on it. The drink he gave her made her cough and she pushed it away, asking instead for water.

There was a throbbing soreness all over her and when Roseanna fluttered in and fussed ineffectively round her, she wished she would go away. The secretary's attentiveness was so clearly aimed at impressing the chief librarian rather than achieving anything of material value that Carolyn, in pain though she was, wanted to laugh out loud. But Richard's attention was so firmly riveted on the chairman's niece and not, to Roseanna's chagrin, on her at all, that she stalked out, head in air.

Graham came in. 'Most unfortunate, Richard,' he muttered. 'That step-stool should have been replaced long ago.'

'My dear chap, do you think I haven't tried to tell her uncle that? One step-ladder for the whole lending section, no properly equipped rest room, not even a staff room. . . .'

Carolyn stirred. Graham walked across and took her hand. 'Feeling better?'

She managed a smile. 'A little, thanks.'

Richard sat on the arm of her chair and Graham moved away. 'That was a stupid thing to do, Carolyn,' Richard murmured, smiling down at her and resting his arm along the back of the chair. 'You're not by any chance suffering from a hangover after last night?'

She smiled up at him, stirred by inexpressibly sweet memories of their kiss. Then she flushed and turned away. Graham stood in the doorway. He was watching them intently and there seemed suddenly to be a heavy sadness about him, like a man who had just come face to face with an inescapable truth. He turned slowly and went from the room.

Carolyn lifted her hand and touched her head. Richard touched it too.

'Painful?' he asked. 'Aches and pains all over?'

She nodded ruefully. 'I'll be covered with bruises tomorrow, I expect.'

He looked concerned. 'Would you like me to call a doctor?'

'No, please don't. There's no need. I'll be back to

normal soon, I'm sure.' She looked up at him uncertainly. 'Mr. Hindon?' He raised his eyebrows. 'Just before I fell, you said you wanted to see me. What about?'

He took a plait between his fingers and stroked it thoughtfully. 'To tell you I'd changed my mind about your tackling a book display.'

'You mean—you'll allow me to do it?'

He smiled at her pleasure. 'At least I can let you try.'

'It's very kind of you to change your mind.'

'Kind?' He didn't like the word. 'Kindness isn't one of my virtues.' He dropped the plait and got up at last. 'No, let's say that I never like to quench initiative and enthusiasm. They're both too rare to be pushed aside and should be—cherished whenever they're found.'

She smiled. 'Even in the chairman's niece?'

He looked at her quickly, walked across and leaned over her, resting his hands on the arms of her chair. His eyes explored her face and he said softly, 'Yes, even in the chairman's niece.'

Roseanna's telephone rang and he straightened. Her raised voice came through the half-open door. '*What?* He's coming up?' The receiver was slammed down and she rushed in.

'Mr. Hindon, he's here. Alderman Bullman's on his way.'

CHAPTER EIGHT

THERE was no knock to announce his entry. He walked straight in. He did not notice his niece at first. As she looked at him before he became aware of her, and saw the belligerence and obstinacy which he wore like a well-loved suit of clothes, she realised with a shock that if he had not been her uncle, she would not have liked him.

Despite the fact that he regarded her as his 'own flesh and blood', she felt no sense of belonging to this man who stalked through life blustering and bludgeoning others into accepting his opinions and his ideas. As she watched him, she analysed her feelings and found a certain resentment against him, closely shadowed by a sense of guilt at her lack of gratitude for his beneficence to her.

Austin Bullman directed a brief greeting towards the chief librarian, who acknowledged it with an unsmiling nod. He looked irritably about him for a chair and saw his niece.

'My lass,' he started towards her, 'what's up? Are you ill?'

She glanced uncertainly at Richard, seeking guidance as to how much she should tell him, but he was staring at his blotter.

'I—I fell down, Uncle.' She saw that he required a further explanation. 'I was on a stool and I fell sideways.'

Austin looked accusingly at Richard. 'Have you had the doctor to her?'

'Miss Lyle considered it unnecessary, Alderman Bullman.'

'But it was up to you to decide. You're in charge. Aren't you?' The question was clearly intended to cast some doubt on the answer.

'Your niece is an adult. I have no power to force her to see a doctor if she refuses.'

Austin Bullman blustered, momentarily the loser. 'What's she doing in here? Isn't there somewhere more comfortable——?'

Richard replied quietly, 'Unfortunately, we have no rest room which could be used for emergencies such as this. Nor do we possess even a staff room. I've raised the matter repeatedly; I've suggested ways of converting various rooms in this building or even putting up an extension at the back. But these suggestions have never even been put to the committee, let alone considered by them. Like so many of my ideas, these have been vetoed —by you—at the source.'

Austin glanced at Carolyn, saw her eyes were closed and made a quick decision. Obviously his niece wasn't interested—wasn't even listening. He pulled up the chair Richard had offered him, drew some papers from his briefcase and spread them on Richard's desk.

'Your agenda for the next committee meeting—I got it through the post this morning. Now,' his finger ran down the numbered items, 'here. This is the one. More book amnesties to get readers to return missing books without threats of heavy fines. I don't agree with it, I don't agree at all.'

Richard also glanced at Carolyn, saw her apparent disinterest and answered, 'Alderman Bullman, I regard my job as that of an educator, not as a member of the police force. It's not our job to seek out criminals with a view to punishing them, or to be vindictive for the sake of it. If we can persuade those who fail to return books at the proper time to bring them back without fear of recrimination, then the library service would benefit by the vast quantity of goodwill which would have accrued in our favour, and our stocks would experience a sudden and very pleasing increase.'

Austin shook his head. 'It looks to me mighty like

you're falling over backwards to protect the culprits. No, young man, the only way to get action in this world is to threaten punishment. Then people will jump to it, mark my words.'

Richard seemed to be having a struggle with his temper.

'And look at these items,' the chairman went on. 'You don't want much, do you? Book lift to save time and effort. Improved lighting in the lending section, more up-to-date shelving. A more efficient heating system. You want to lengthen the period of loan from two to three weeks. You want more staff. Why? Answer me that!'

'Yes, I will. Take the growth factor into account. A good library, a living library, is growing all the time. Therefore an organisation which has been run satisfactorily in the past with a dozen assistants will not be able to operate successfully with even double that number if the growth of a library has trebled. This library has grown—it was growing even before I took over. I have been into this thoroughly with my deputy and the answer is—we need more staff, and unless we get them, we simply cannot operate efficiently, either now or in the future.'

'Tell that one to the marines, young man! In my opinion, you've got all the staff you'll need for a long time to come. I don't agree with all your ideas. This place has been run properly for years on what's here, and no one has convinced me, or ever will, that all this "modern" nonsense is any more efficient than the well-tried and proven old methods.' He stood up, prepared to end the discussion.

'Alderman Bullman,' Richard faced him squarely across the desk, 'if you tell me that all these alterations and improvements I'm suggesting are out of the question, taking into account the age of this building——'

'I didn't say that,' Austin blustered. 'Don't put words into my mouth, young man.'

'—then give me a new library—properly designed and purpose-built, that's all I ask.'

'Ask away, young man, but you won't get. The money's just not there. Even if you got it through the library committee, you wouldn't get it through the finance committee.'

'But, Alderman Bullman,' Richard persisted, 'you're on the finance committee as well as the library committee. Wouldn't it be in your power to help it through?'

Austin spluttered, red in the face, and temporarily robbed of words, 'I haven't time to waste on this nonsense.' He looked at Carolyn. 'I'm taking you home, lass.'

Carolyn stirred. 'No, thank you, Uncle.'

'Look, lass, you've had a nasty fall, from the sound of it. You won't lose your job just because you take the day off, will she, Mr. Librarian?' Even his way of addressing Richard was insulting. He gave Richard a taunting 'answer that one' grin, but Carolyn said again,

'No, thanks. I'll be all right in a few minutes, then I'll go back to my work.'

He shrugged his heavy shoulders, bent down and kissed her cheek and went out. There was a long silence. Richard rested his elbows on the desk and stared at his hands. 'Perhaps he's wondering whether or not to choke me,' Carolyn thought miserably.

At last he said, 'You could have gone with him. We wouldn't have missed your services. Someone else could easily do your job.'

'That,' she whispered, 'is a polite way of saying I'm not wanted.' She swallowed the lump in her throat and went on, 'I don't blame you for hating me. Everywhere I go I must remind you of my uncle. It's obvious I'll have to relieve you of my presence for good before long. Somehow I'll have to talk my uncle round to my point of view.'

Richard didn't say, 'I want you to stay. You're doing better here than I expected.' His absence of response distressed her, but she told herself she was a fool. The man had vowed right from the start that he would get rid of her.

He came to life at last. 'You'll have to go home, you know. After a fall like that, you must rest for today at least.' He seemed to come to a decision. 'I'll get Graham to take you. You'd like that, wouldn't you?'

'I'd rather you took me,' she wanted to say, but nodded. At Richard's summons, Graham appeared. He said jokingly that he would be delighted to put his car at Carolyn's disposal and pulled her gently from her chair. He put his arm round her, saying, 'This will give you more support. How do the legs feel?'

She walked a few paces. 'Not too bad. It's my side and my head that got the worst of it.'

He patted his shoulder. 'There's this to rest on, if you feel so inclined.'

Richard watched them. 'Don't come in tomorrow, Miss Lyle, if you're still not fit. I'd hate you to pass out and then have your uncle down on us like a ton of bricks again, demanding another explanation.'

She heard the sarcasm, but sought nevertheless for an accompanying smile. It was missing.

In the car she tried to relax, but an impulse made her say, 'I heard my uncle in action today. It was even worse than I expected.' She rested her head on the back of the seat.

'Your moment of truth?'

'In a way, yes. But I've never been under any illusion about him, despite his past kindnesses to me.' She sighed. 'I don't know how Mr. Hindon can keep his temper with him.'

'My dear, if he lost it, things would go against him even more than they do now. His only weapon is dogged persistence and he's got plenty of that.' He laughed shortly. 'But he can't get rough with the committee chairman.'

'No,' Carolyn agreed bitterly, her voice full of tears, 'only with the chairman's niece.'

Graham gave her a compassionate glance. 'Richard gets so fed up at times that he takes matters into his own hands.' He looked at her again, with alarm this time. 'But for heaven's sake don't tell your uncle, will you?' She assured him that she wouldn't.

'That notice board in the lending section, for instance—Richard's been asking for a new one ever since he came—he even put it in the estimates. But no go, it was knocked out by—guess who? The chairman himself.'

He drew up outside her house. 'So Richard's getting the building department of the local technical college to make one and he's taking the money out of the library's book fund. Strictly not done, and it's not a thing I'd do—I wouldn't have the nerve—but I don't blame him.'

He saw her to the front door. 'Will you be all right? Your gran in?'

'She's out till tea-time, but I'll manage.'

'Take it easy for the rest of the day, my dear.' She was searching for the key. 'Carolyn?' She looked up at him and his eyes raked her face like a man taking final leave of something infinitely precious. 'Goodbye, Carolyn.' Swiftly he kissed her on the lips and left her.

That evening, Carolyn rested on the couch. Her grandmother fussed round her anxiously, refusing to let her help in any way.

'Just you sit there, dear. Your uncle's calling in later. He's off somewhere again tomorrow.'

'Gran, he—he came to the library this morning, while I was resting in Mr. Hindon's room. It was awful hearing them arguing, Gran.'

'Well, I expect your uncle was right, dear.'

'But, Gran, he was wrong about—well, almost everything. Only he couldn't see it. He's so—so dogmatic. He won't listen to anyone else.'

When she saw her grandmother's face, she wondered if she had gone too far in her criticism, because her grandmother worshipped Austin almost as an oracle.

'But, Carolyn dear, he knows what he's talking about.'

'Of course he does, Gran,' she said gently, 'in his own line. But Mr. Hindon's an expert. He's highly qualified—he's a Fellow of the Library Association. Where librarianship's concerned, he knows what he's talking about more than Uncle does.' She avoided her grandmother's scandalised eyes and went on desperately, 'Gran, can't you tell Uncle to try to help Mr. Hindon, instead of always standing in his way?'

'But, dear, no one can tell Austin what to do. I've never dared to, myself. Ever since he was a little boy, he seems somehow to have known best.'

Carolyn sighed. She was up against her grandmother's blind spot and knew she was wasting her time.

Suddenly her grandmother asked, 'You like Mr. Hindon, dear?'

'Yes, very much, Gran. But,' she whispered, because tears threatened, 'he doesn't like me.'

She looked up, alarmed at what she had given away, and found her grandmother looking at her with surprise and speculation.

'Oh dear,' she said, bustling out of the room, 'oh dear, oh dear. . . .'

Austin arrived, his manner as usual bumptious and belligerent. He started straight away on Richard Hindon. 'You heard me, lass, putting that Mr. Librarian in his place this morning. I have to keep him down there,' he pressed the air with his thumb, 'otherwise he'd be too uppity for words.'

'But, Uncle,' something was driving her on, and she

ignored the restraint her brain was struggling to impose on her words, 'as I told Gran, he's an expert, he knows what he's doing just as much as you do in your own line of business.' She shut her eyes to his horrified look and pressed on. 'You drive him so far sometimes, Uncle, that he doesn't wait for your permission. He just goes ahead and does things.' She rushed on, her praise growing more lavish as her uncle's expression grew more horrified. 'He's got so many wonderful ideas that it must be terrible never being able to put them into practice, because of—because you. . . .'

'What's this I'm hearing now, eh?' Austin took her up at once. 'He "just goes ahead and does them", does he? What does that mean, eh?'

She knew she had gone too far. In her efforts to help the man she loved, she had betrayed him. She had done what he had always said she would do—she had let him down, acted as a spy, given away his secrets to the enemy.

In the end, her uncle got the details out of her. 'I'm going off for a few days. But I'll be having a few words with Mr. Richard Hindon when I get back. While I'm away, I'll be thinking up just what I'm going to say to that clever young puppy!' He slammed out of the house.

That night in bed, Carolyn despaired. She trembled at what would happen when her uncle confronted Richard with her allegations. She would not be able to speak a word in her own defence and she would have to take everything he cared to give. She turned over, trying to sleep, but it would not come.

She thought about Graham. How much did he know of her feelings for Richard? Had he guessed her secret? Recalling his kiss that morning as he had left her, as though he was saying 'goodbye', she knew that he had.

Carolyn returned to work next day. Her limbs were stiff with bruises, her head still tender, but she managed the clerical jobs which Keith gave her, because they did not involve moving about.

Richard was out all day. During the afternoon, Hilary breezed in, leaving her children in the entrance porch. Carolyn took her into the store room to talk. Hilary said she was sorry to hear about Carolyn's fall. Richard had told her.

'You don't look too bad, though.'

Carolyn laughed. 'The real damage doesn't show. It's hidden under my clothes.'

Hilary put her hand on Carolyn's arm. 'I've come to ask you a favour. Turn it down if you want, but on Monday—you know it's the Bank Holiday?—I've promised to take the kids to the Devil's Dyke. So, going all maternally attentive—not usually my line—I've got to keep my promise. But I can't face the prospect of coping alone, and anyway, Basi keeps asking for "Caroly". Would you be a pet? My darling brother won't come. He's out so much now anyway that I begin to wonder if he's got a woman at last.' She lowered her voice. 'It's probably that secretary of his. I've seen them out together once or twice.'

Carolyn battled with the tightening of her body. She mustn't show Hilary how much she cared. 'I've got nothing else to do on Monday. I'd probably just moon around at home, so—yes, I'd love to come.'

They arranged a time for Carolyn to call and Hilary left. 'So Roseanna's strategy's working, is it?' Carolyn thought miserably, as she tried to concentrate on her work. 'Easy does it, I suppose. Softly, softly. . . . Then move in for the kill.'

Carolyn and Pearl went home together that evening. Carolyn could detect an unusual lightness in Pearl's tone of voice, and there was a glow in her features which touched them with a fleeting beauty.

'You look happy, Pearl.'

'Do I? Perhaps I am.' Then it came out as though she could not hold it back. 'Mr. Cotes—Graham—has asked me out. I'm having a meal with him tomorrow evening, then we're going to a film.'

After the first shock—she acknowledged secretly afterwards that it was a flick of jealousy—Carolyn said how glad she was to hear it.

'You're made for each other, and it's time you both realised it!'

Monday afternoon was unusually warm and sunny. It was late May and holiday crowds packed the promenades and beaches. Carolyn watched them from the top of the bus that was taking her to Hilary's house. She knew Richard would be out. She hadn't bothered to dress up and was wearing lightweight pink slacks and a thin white sleeveless blouse. She carried her jacket over her arm.

When she arrived, Hilary greeted her looking unkempt and white-faced. She put a hand to her head. 'Sorry, dear, the Dyke trip's off. This headache's giving me hell. But come in, do.'

'Why can't we go?' Helen whined, irritating her mother. 'Now Carolyn's come, why can't she take us?'

'For goodness' sake, Helen, be quiet! She's been driving me mad,' Hilary told Carolyn, 'ever since I said I couldn't go.'

'Of course I'll take you, Helen,' Carolyn said. 'I'd be as disappointed as you if we didn't go, darling.'

'But, Carolyn——' Hilary protested.

'It's all right, Hilary, I'll manage them. And it would give you a chance to rest. You look all in.'

'Thanks for the sympathy. My dear brother said it served me right, I shouldn't lead such a "gay" life. He said I needed sobering up. Honestly!' she tutted. 'Sometimes I regret ever having asked him to stay here while Clive's away.'

Carolyn changed the subject swiftly. 'We'll have tea somewhere——'

'Oh, it's all right—I've made sandwiches and so on. We were going to picnic.'

'That's fine, then. Let's pack them in something and we'll be off.'

Hilary waved them down the road towards the bus stop and closed the door with a thankful snap. The bus was crowded and Helen insisted on going upstairs. Carolyn struggled with the push-chair which she lifted into the luggage compartment, then carried Basi up the stairs.

The bus wound its way up and up, along the roads which cut across the Downs. In the distance the coast-line was broken by high buildings—multi-storey flats and hotels, church spires and power stations.

The bus was nearing the end of its climb and a car came past. From their seats upstairs they looked down on it as it pulled out to the offside to overtake and the driver seemed for a fleeting moment to be searching the bus for someone he knew. Then the car sped on.

'Uncle Rich!' Helen cried, staring at the fast-disappearing vehicle. 'That was Uncle Rich. He's come to find us!'

'Unker Rich,' echoed Basi, 'want Unker Rich.'

Carolyn's pulses leapt and faltered and steadied again. Of course the children were wrong. 'It couldn't be, darling. He's out somewhere else.'

'But it was,' Helen insisted. 'That was his car. You just see.'

As the bus drew up at the terminus outside the Devil's Dyke Hotel, Carolyn scanned the parked cars, half in fear, half in hope, for Richard Hindon. He was there, leaning on his elbow against the side of his car, watching the passengers alight one by one.

Helen broke away and ran across the road. 'Uncle Rich, I saw you! We were on the bus, and I knew it was you. Carolyn wouldn't believe me.'

'Clever girl,' said Richard laconically, 'I always said you were intelligent.'

'Unker Rich!' Basi shouted, pulling at Carolyn's slacks as she struggled to open the push-chair. Richard strolled across the road and took it from her. He flipped it open and lifted Basi into it.

'Thank you,' Carolyn said, her tone ungracious.

'That's what I came for—to help. Where's the bag with the sandwiches in my sister said she gave you?'

Carolyn handed it to him. 'There was no need for you to come,' she muttered sullenly, trying to persuade herself she felt no excitement at his unexpected appearance. 'Unless once again you didn't trust me with your sister's children.'

He shot her an amused look. 'What do you want me to answer? That I trust you implicitly under all circumstances? If so, then I'm sorry, I couldn't say it with conviction.'

'You needn't have come,' she snapped, forcibly taking the push-chair from him and pushing Basi herself. 'I was looking forward to a pleasant afternoon.'

'And now I'm here, it's unpleasant, is that it?'

She didn't answer and turned her attention to the children.

'Can I have an ice cream?' Helen asked, spotting the sign outside the shop.

'Ice c'eam,' Basi echoed, leaping up and down in his seat.

Richard pushed his hand into his pocket and jingled some money. 'Want one?' he asked Carolyn, who shook her head.

'All right,' said Richard, 'be the odd one out.'

He took Helen into the shop and Carolyn wished she had said "yes". She would have loved an ice cream. She pushed Basi over the road and gazed at the breathtaking view across the Weald. It stretched for many miles into the hazy distance, field upon field, green merging with gold and brown, geometrically patterned but predominantly rectangular, raised here and there like quilting, bounded by hedgerows and scattered with villages, churches and woods.

Richard, leading Helen across the road, disturbed

157

Carolyn's reverie. He gave Basi his ice cream and pushed one into Carolyn's hand. 'I knew you really wanted one,' he grinned.

She thanked him sourly and he started on his own ice cream. After a while, he commented, 'Beautiful view.' She nodded. 'We're about seven hundred feet up at this point, but there,' he pointed towards the west, 'is Chanctonbury Ring, and that's nearly eight hundred feet up.'

'I know,' she told him, 'I've lived here for years.'

He raised his eyebrows at her ill temper, but went on, 'Ever climbed up there? It's hard going getting to the top, but it's worth the effort. You get a view stretching for thirty miles across more than half a dozen counties. Those beech trees form a circle—hence its name—and were specially planted two centuries ago. They stand inside the mounds of an Iron Age earthwork.' He grinned. 'I'll lend you a book on Sussex some time. My personal stock of books is limitless.' He was busy with his ice cream. 'And what's more, I'm not vindictive. I don't impose a fine if they're not returned on time. I conduct a permanent amnesty where my own books are concerned.' He shot her a quick, mocking look. 'Don't tell your uncle that, will you!'

He finished his ice cream, threw the wrapping paper into a litter bin and pointed eastwards. 'If it weren't for the trees and the curve of the hills, you could see Ditchling Beacon, the highest point of the Downs. That, in case you don't know, is eight hundred and eighteen feet high. There was once a great forest there called Anderida. It had dangerous animals wandering about in it.' He smiled provocatively. 'Even more dangous than I am.'

She looked at him, saw his broad smile, felt his magnetism which, in his present devil-may-care mood, was overpowering. She wanted him to open his arms for her to run into them, to hold her as he had on the night of Hilary's party. She moved away, her heart racing.

'Over there,' he was saying, his arm swinging north-wards and coming to rest on her shoulders, 'are the North Downs. Their highest point is Leith Hill which, on a clear day, is visible from here. So there are prob-ably people over there many miles away staring at us as we're staring at them. Now,' he suggested, 'I think it's time we moved on. The Dyke itself is this way.' He took the push-chair from Carolyn's hands and propelled it across the road, with the others following.

They stood at the end of the great valley which formed the Devil's Dyke, its name coming from past legends.

'Every time I come here, it takes my breath away for a few moments,' Carolyn said.

'I agree it's beautiful. If I may sound like a textbook again, geological this time, I'll tell you how it was formed.' He smiled. 'Tell me when you want to shut the book. Between the Ice Ages, experts think it's probable that the water level in the chalk of the Downs was high enough to keep the rivers flowing, so a river valley developed. They also think it's likely that melting water from a local ice cap on the Downs escaped through this valley to deepen it into the present gorge. Now it's one of the many dry valleys in the area and, I think, one of the most spectacular. Lecture over. Let's go down into the dyke itself.'

They made their way over the bumps in the uneven ground, through the long grass and down the path which wound its way between the steep slopes of the valley sides. Carolyn raised her eyes to the top where the gorse-speckled slopes met the sky, and felt some-thing like awe stirring inside her.

They found a quiet spot and spread out their coats. Helen put herself between Carolyn and Richard and Basi sat in his push-chair, facing them. Carolyn pro-duced the neat packets of sandwiches and handed them round. Richard rested sideways on his elbow and ate in silence, his gaze roaming round and returning now and then to his companions. Carolyn, glancing at him, found his eyes on her. He smiled and looked away again, seeming perfectly content and utterly in tune with his surroundings.

She could not understand why he had come. Was his secretary engaged elsewhere and he, having nothing better to do, had volunteered to come chasing after them in place of his sister?

Tea over, Carolyn packed the remaining food away and picked up their litter. Richard was lying full length, next to her now that Helen had moved. His hand covered his eyes and he seemed to be asleep. Taking courage from the fact, Carolyn lay back, too, pillowing her head on her hands. The sun warmed her through, the children's voices drifted over her and she relaxed into contentment.

A slight movement from Richard brought her back into acute awareness of him and she tensed, but he had only moved his hand to brush off an insect. She sat up, unable to get back to her relaxed state. Feeling the almost tangible pull of him, she had to get away.

The children had strayed a short distance along the valley and she stood up, intending to follow them. Richard opened his eyes and watched her, but still he said nothing. As she moved away, he covered his eyes again. He seemed completely indifferent to her presence, and she could have cried at his lack of interest.

Helen started climbing. Basi tried to follow, but his legs refused to lift him more than a few inches, so he flopped down and watched.

'Carolyn, I bet you can't climb as high as I can,' Helen challenged.

'Can't I?' Carolyn called. 'Just you wait and see!'

She half-ran, half-walked up the incline after the little girl and caught her up some distance ahead. She was gasping for breath and stood for a moment, looking down. Richard had got up and was watching them, hands on hips.

'How d'you think you're going to get down?' he called, cupping his hands to make the sound carry. 'It's steeper than you think.' But they ignored him and pressed on.

'Come back, you stupid girls!' he shouted. 'Carolyn, tell Helen to stop. She's too young to know what she's doing.'

So he's putting me in my place, Carolyn thought sulkily. The role of nanny, governess, the simple-minded nursemaid.

'Go down now, darling,' she told Helen. 'Uncle Rich is getting worried about you.'

'All right, but you come, too.' Carolyn had to agree, but against her will, because she wanted to show Richard Hindon that she was able to take care of herself.

Slowly they began to go down and, as Richard had warned them, it was a difficult descent. As they neared the bottom, Helen began to run.

'Uncle Rich,' she yelled, 'catch me! I can't stop. I'll fall!'

He stood at the base of the slope and as the child raced downwards and began to slip, he caught her, swung her round and put her down. She wandered away to join Basi.

Carolyn came to a halt. He laughed up at her, arms folded, waiting. 'Now you?' he called.

'Not on your life,' she shouted back. 'I'm not a six-year-old. I can stand on my own two feet.' And she continued her descent.

Her legs began to turn traitor, her footsteps speeded up and she found herself running as Helen had done. She grew frightened as she lost control over their speed.

'Richard!' she shrieked, '*Richard*! Catch me or I'll fall. . . .'

He ran a few steps up the slope to meet her and she fell into his arms. The impetus of her body pulled them down and they rolled to the bottom of the slope.

They lay still, locked together.

He raised his head, stared into her eyes, then brought his mouth down on hers with a possessive and relentless pressure. She could not resist him any more. As the kiss went on, she gave herself up to the ecstasy of it, and became uncaring as to how much he would read into her surrender. If he knew now that she loved him, there was nothing she could do about it.

He lifted his head at last, but stayed where he was. He held her eyes and she struggled to find something to say.

'Thank you,' she whispered, 'for catching me.'

'Oh,' he answered, grinning, 'think nothing of it. I always catch a woman when she throws herself at me.'

'Yes,' she said, still breathless, 'but you needn't have——'

'Kissed you? Oh, I always kiss a woman when she falls into my arms. Especially a beautiful one. It's a habit I've developed over the years.'

He was laughing at her as though the devil himself had entered into him and she tried to struggle free.

'It's no use, you won't get away until I choose to release you.' His eyes wandered over her face, flushed and vital, beneath him. 'Has anyone told you how beautiful you are?' She didn't answer because she knew he was mocking her. 'I expect your boy-friend has.' He traced her eyebrows. 'What would he say if he could see you now—being unfaithful to him?'

She made a frenzied but unsuccessful attempt to escape. 'What are you talking about?' she cried.

'Oh, don't worry. I expect it of a woman. I've watched my sister being unfaithful to her husband....'

'I'm sure she's never gone that far.'

'No? Well, perhaps not, but I'm sure she's had a damned good try.' He lowered his voice and narrowed his eyes. 'I wonder how far you would go in your unfaithfulness?'

The voices of the children brought them back to their surroundings. 'They're coming,' she hissed. 'Now will you let me go?'

'Maybe I will,' he drawled, releasing her slowly. 'Otherwise they'll see us and tell their mother.' He lay back and lifted his hands behind his head. 'Then she'd come to the conclusion that I'm human after all. And that would never do.'

She sat up, smoothing her hair and trying to calm herself, fighting off the pain and the misery. His baiting words, his worldly cynicism, his unwavering mistrust of her sickened her beyond words.

She would never please this man, no matter how hard she tried. Because of her relationship to the man he hated, she would never gain his trust.

'Are we going?' Helen asked. 'Mummy said we mustn't be late back.'

Richard got up lazily and held out his hand to Carolyn. She put hers into his with reluctance and he pulled her up to face him. He smiled into her eyes, but she turned away and picked up her coat.

Helen took over the push-chair and walked ahead with Basi. Richard's arm went round Carolyn's waist and they walked together like lovers. They drew indulgent smiles from passers-by and Carolyn said bitterly, 'The irony of it is that we must look like one big happy family. If only people knew!'

Richard laughed loudly. Then he pulled her closer and whispered, 'Forgiven me?'

'What for? The kiss?'

'The *kiss*? Not on your life! I don't ask to be forgiven for something which was so obviously—er—mutually enjoyable. No, I meant for coming with you.'

She shrugged. 'What difference would it make whether I've forgiven you or not?'

He tutted, 'Prevaricating. Just like a woman. Never give a straight answer.'

'They were right,' she said, almost to herself, 'when

163

they said you hated women.'

He laughed again. 'Is that what they say about me? You know,' he slanted a look at her, 'they could be right. Stupid creatures, most of them.'

She twisted free and said grimly to Helen, 'I'll push Basi now.'

Helen skipped to her uncle's side and took his hand.

'Somebody loves me,' commented Richard, with a grin, showing Carolyn his niece's hand in his. But Helen soon tired of that and took over the push-chair again. Richard held up his empty hand. 'It's getting cold. It needs a woman's touch to warm it up.'

'Pity you haven't got your girl-friend with you, then.' The bitter words were out before she could stop them.

He looked puzzled. 'What girl-friend? Enlighten me.'

'Your secretary,' she snapped.

'Oh, I—see,' he said slowly, then smiled broadly. 'Yes, it is a pity Roseanna isn't with me. Never mind, You'll do.' He seized her hand and held it prisoner.

They walked in silence behind Helen and Basi, and Carolyn remembered with a shock what would happen next day when her uncle returned. He would demand to see Richard and challenge him about the notice board. And after that, Richard would never want to hold her hand again.

Involuntarily her fingers tightened round his and he glanced at her curiously. They were almost at the end of the Dyke valley, only a few minutes from the car park.

Richard put his hands on her shoulders and turned her to face him. Slowly, so slowly—giving her time to refuse if she had wanted—his mouth approached hers. She knew she should break away before it happened, but she also knew that it would be the last time he would ever kiss her. She raised her lips to meet his and withheld nothing from the kiss they exchanged. As they drew apart, his eyes searched hers, his expression

164

serious, troubled almost, and his arm rested across her shoulders as they approached the car.

'Still testing me,' she whispered when she was capable of speech, 'to discover how far I'll go?'

'Perhaps,' he answered, a little abrupt.

He took her home and they all waved as she stood on the doorstep watching them drive away.

CHAPTER NINE

CAROLYN was in the store room when her uncle arrived. He did not ask for her, but stormed straight up the stairs, leaving behind a havoc of questioning glances. As time passed, she wondered what they were saying in the librarian's room. What did Richard Hindon think of her now? Did he regret the kisses he seemed so ready to give her yesterday? What would he say—and do—after her uncle had gone?

She grew desperate with fear, she tried to think up answers to imaginary questions, she sought ways of clearing herself, but was forced at last to admit that her guilt was indisputable and could not be explained away.

Some time later, her uncle left. He passed her by without even seeing her. Her heart was throbbing painfully and her ears were attuned to the ring of the internal telephone summoning her to the chief librarian. But no message came. When she could not stand the suspense any longer, she decided to go to him. Somehow she had to explain what had happened, to make some attempt to clear herself.

She went into his secretary's office. It was empty, so she decided to wait. She could hear Roseanna's voice in Richard's room and knew they must be talking about her by the savage way Richard was speaking.

The inner door opened and Roseanna saw her. 'Yes, Miss Lyle?' she asked coldly.

'Can I—is it possible to see Mr. Hindon?'

Roseanna withdrew into Richard's room and closed the door. She returned, saying, 'Mr. Hindon doesn't wish to see you.'

Carolyn ran her tongue round her lips. 'But I——' She had never expected this. A storm of abuse, perhaps, angry words, threats even, but not this. 'Please?' she said, almost pleading, and hating herself for doing so. 'Please ask him again.'

Roseanna disappeared and when she returned, held the door open, indicating that Carolyn could go in. 'He said only for a few minutes.'

He barely raised his head as she stood in front of him. 'Well?'

'I've—I've come to say I'm sorry. You won't believe me, but I am.' No response from him. 'I didn't intend to tell my uncle anything,' he moved irritably, 'but he was saying such awful things about you, I—I—well, it slipped out.' Still no response. 'I said it to—to prove to him how wrong he was in treating you so badly....' She tailed off, feeling she was talking to herself.

He raised weary eyes. 'Have you finished?' He looked at his watch. 'I have an appointment.'

'Mr. Hindon, he said to me once that it wouldn't be long before you became a member of the Establishment.' She seemed at last to be capturing his attention. 'He said that he would make things so difficult for you, you would give up in despair and stop fighting them and join them. Then they'd have no more trouble with you. That's why he's doing all this.'

Now she had his full interest. He was leaning back with an incredulous smile on his face. '*I*—become an Establishment man? Is that what he hopes?' He thumped his desk. 'Over my dead body. Tell him that from me, will you?' He narrowed his eyes as he contemplated her. 'This "spy" system—it seems to work both ways. I could "use" you, as Graham once suggested. I could feed you with my ideas and get you to pass them on to him. With your "loyalty" to me, as you once so touchingly put it, you could work on him and get round him my behalf.'

Now she used his words. She dragged them out. 'Have you finished?'

Roseanna put her head round the door. 'Richard,

167

your appointment.'

Carolyn knew it was a prearranged signal to get her out of the room. She went.

One evening in mid-June, Carolyn had promised to baby-sit for Hilary, but when she arrived, Hilary told her she had changed her mind.

'I'll have an early night instead. Thanks a lot, though, for coming. What will you do—go back home?'

Carolyn looked out at the warm evening sun, felt a longing for the freedom of the Downs. 'I'll go for a walk. Get some fresh air.'

As Hilary opened the front door to let her out, Carolyn glanced up the stairs. 'Richard's in,' Hilary told her. 'Did you want to see him?'

Hastily she shook her head.

Hilary walked with her to the gate. 'Lovely evening,' she said. 'If I stay out here much longer, I might decide to go with you.' She waved and went in.

The air was soft and caressing high up on the Downs. The hills, dappled with gorse and shrubs, rose and fell into the distance, crisscrossed by well-worn paths, hollowed here and there by great coombes indented into the hillsides, cupping their own shadows. To the south and far away was the sea, blue-grey in the evening sun.

Carolyn leaned against a concrete post, part of a fence erected to keep cattle and horses enclosed. She stared ahead, lost to everything but the misery of her own thoughts. She had not spoken to Richard for a long time. She had seen him in the library, but he had not been near her. Graham had kept away, too. She supposed he had had his orders. After all, he had once let something slip, so there must be no danger of that happening again.

She heard footsteps, but did not look round. People often went up there, walking their dogs.

'Carolyn?' A man was standing beside her. Her head

jerked round. Richard. She said nothing, just walked on. He walked with her. He was at her side and her heart was almost breaking.

'I'm tired,' she said at last, and sat down beside a bush, hoping he would walk on. But he stopped and sat beside her. As she turned her head away, her plaits caught in the gorse and she tugged at them. They would not come.

'These stupid plaits,' she blurted out, 'these *stupid* plaits!' and tugged harder. There were tears in her eyes now with the pain from pulling.

Richard stretched across and patiently untangled them. 'You must like them, otherwise you wouldn't have them, would you?'

'Why are you here?' she snapped. 'I didn't invite you. Unless,' she added acidly, 'you've suddenly developed some deep down need of a woman's company. Any woman, even me.'

He laughed cynically. 'I? Have a need of women? I have no need of women in my life.' He settled himself back on the ground. 'I have the awful example of my sister in front of my eyes all the time. After experiencing her and discovering through observation that she's representative of her kind, she's put me off the opposite sex for the rest of my life.'

Surely he must know he was hurting her, so why was he saying it? To warn her off? To put her back in her place as a mere working acquaintance?

'You're impossible, quite impossible,' she snapped.

'I know. That's why I've never taken a wife. I walk alone, I'm a solitary, and as such I'd be impossible to live with.'

She tore a piece of bracken to pieces. 'No woman would ever tolerate you,' she said viciously.

He said levelly, 'You're absolutely right. I'm aware of my own limitations.'

So it was a warning after all. She threw down the

remains of the bracken, brushed her hands, stood up and walked away. She reached a gate and leaned against it, raking the distant horizon until it blurred and distorted and disappeared. She searched blindly for a handkerchief and dabbed at her eyes.

She walked on and after a while, glanced back. Richard was leaning on the gate she had left, staring at the line of the sea. She climbed a stile and as she did so saw that he was following her. He was walking slowly some distance away and plainly had no intention of catching her up.

Her eyes followed the curving, twisting flight of a bird. As it rose higher and disappeared, she wished she could break free of her surroundings and go after it, released from the misery of her heartbreak, the hopeless love that imprisoned her like a cage.

She went home by bus and stared in the dressing-table mirror. Her mind, in the desperation of her unhappiness, turned destructively inwards. She hated herself, her face, everything about her. She would shake off the fetters of the past, of the present, and most of all of her own personality. Something would have to go. She jerked her plaits forward. These would have to go. Tomorrow—it was her afternoon off—she would have her hair cut and nothing would make her change her mind. Nothing did.

The hairdresser looked uncertainly at the pale gold curtain she had been told to cut down. 'Are you sure?' she asked. 'You want me to take it all off?'

Carolyn, wishing the girl would stop dithering, said firmly, 'Absolutely sure. I'm sick of it.' She nearly added, 'And all that it stands for.'

'It's so beautiful,' the girl persisted, 'it must have taken years. . . .' Then she sighed and started cutting. Afterwards it lay in silken strands on the floor.

It was over. In her room again, defiant, lightheaded with a vicious sort of triumph, her hand explored the emptiness of the back of her neck. When her grandmother had greeted her on the doorstep, she had almost cried.

'Oh, my dearie,' she had moaned, 'what have you done?'

'I've had it cut off, Gran. The lot. Now I'm going to wash it. And thank goodness it won't take so long to dry now.'

She had marched into the bathroom and, without once looking in the mirror, had washed and dried it. Now it curled softly, like a pale gold cap, round her cheeks, and she felt drunk with defiance. She had snapped her fingers in the face of the past. She had broken free.

Her eyes, a little wild still, had fallen on her mother's portrait. She took it up, studied it, saw the softly curling hair, searched her own features. Now there must surely be a likeness, a similarity to this beautiful girl who had been her mother. For a long time she contemplated first the gentle smiling face and then her own. She analysed and made hopeful comparisons. But she gave up in the end. There was no obvious resemblance at all, not even a suggestion of a likeness.

Shane called for her that evening. He staggered backwards as she let him in. This was the sort of reaction, she knew, which she would have to expect for a long time to come.

'My sweet,' he said, his tones sombre, 'if you'd let me know of the passing, I would have gone into mourning, or at least have worn a black band on my arm. What in heaven's name made you do it?' He moaned and became dramatic. 'Those incomparable tresses! Where are they now?'

She didn't tell him she had sold them to the hairdresser. She said, with a smile, 'I suppose you don't want to take me out now? I suppose I'm not decorative enough for you now my distinctive feature has gone?'

He was staring at her still. 'I can't get over it. But,

sweetie, you're just as good to look at. Your face is revealed now in all its glory.'

She laughed at his flowery language and they went out. 'It's a long time, anyway, since I've been honoured with your company,' she said. 'Been trying out pastures new?'

'Er—well, there's a pretty little thing I met at a party, name of Jane——'

'I thought so. I'm relieved really. I thought it might have been a certain Mrs. Hilary Roding.'

'My dear, I'm not an idiot. Even if I'd been so tempted, think how bad for business it would have been. All my respectable clients wanting their big houses and their worthwhile properties would have veered off my firm and gone to the shop next door. I grant you she's—well, cuddly and even tempting, but no, it wouldn't have done at all.' He glanced at her. 'Now, where shall we go?'

She gave him an impish grin. 'Somewhere dark, where, in my shorn state, you can hide me?'

He laughed. 'Now you're being an idiot.'

They saw a film and held hands and laughed a lot. Carolyn knew it was meaningless. They had almost grown up together and it was the past they were trading on. Her heart was elsewhere, and Shane's was all over the place. They both had each other's measure and were the happier together because of it.

Keith exclaimed with the horror she had come to expect when she arrived at the library next day. The others gathered round and expressed their shock and disapproval. At least, she thought, this is getting it all over at once.

'Who sheared you?' Cathy asked. 'Which shepherd —I mean hairdresser—did the dirty deed?'

Carolyn told her and Cathy tutted and muttered 'sacrilege' and 'shouldn't have done it'.

'This book display,' said Keith, motioning Carolyn

into the quiet of the store room, 'have you decided on your main theme?'

'I thought,' Carolyn said, 'that, since it's the height of summer, I'd call it something like "summer gardens" and get out all the books I could find on gardens and gardening.'

'M'm, not bad. Perhaps a better theme for the spring, but for a trial effort, it would do.'

Someone called him. 'Won't be a moment,' he said, and went out.

Carolyn leaned against the table and thought about the design she would use for the poster advertising her book display. There was a movement behind her and she turned. Richard was staring at her hair, his face pale, his eyes stunned.

As she looked at him she knew, with a flash of insight, why she had done it. She had wanted to give him pain, to hurt him as he had hurt her ever since she had known him. And she had succeeded. But the dazed look in his eyes twisted the swift triumph within her into a double-ended sword and his pain became hers. She turned away. She should have known—against this man whom she loved so completely, she could not hope to win.

She forced her lips to life. 'Good morning, Mr. Hindon.'

He seemed, with an effort, to pull himself together. 'Why did you do it?' His voice was lifeless, dead.

'To—to stop you complaining about it.'

'Complain—about your hair?'

'Well,' she became defensive, 'it has at least given you one less thing to hold against me and one less name to call me behind my back.'

'Name? What name?'

'Goldilocks.' It didn't seem so bad now she had said it. Almost a term of affection. . . .

His voice softened. 'Who told you I called you that?'

'Your sister.'

'Yes,' he said, 'she would. Did they—did they give you back your hair after cutting it off?'

'Yes.'

His eyes seemed oddly bright. 'Then you've got it?'

'No. They told me it was—beautiful hair and a most unusual colour. I didn't want it, so—I offered to sell it to them. They bought it.'

'You *sold* it?' Now there was cynicism in his voice. 'Of course, I should have known it was the money you were after.'

Fiercely she turned on him, but he went out.

It was later in the day. She was moving round the shelves looking out the books for her display when Miss Stagg called her over. In a loud whisper she said, 'There's been a message from Mr. Hindon's secretary. He wants to see you. Mrs. Harvey says he's very angry and you must go up straight away.'

The staircase had never seemed so steep, the upstairs corridor so long or so dark as when her heavy footsteps took her towards Richard Hindon's room. She knocked on his door, Roseanna opened it and she went in.

Richard did not tell his secretary to go. His anger was cold, his eyes calculating and cruel. Carolyn's instinct was to turn and run, but pride and knowledge of her innocence of any crime he could charge her with kept her rigid in front of him.

'You've done it again, Miss Lyle,' he said. 'Once again you've acted as spy, passed on information to your uncle.'

She looked at him dully, wishing he would explain what he was talking about. Her lack of response seemed to incense him. 'How you got to know about it I cannot understand. Since the last episode, I have given Graham Cotes strict instructions not to pass on to you any information whatsoever. I myself have been utterly guarded in what I've said to you.'

'Mr. Hindon,' she said quietly, 'I'm sorry, but I don't know what you're talking about.'

'You expect me to believe that? You're trying to pretend that you did not tell your uncle that the lecture room here has been let to a group of young people he looks on with disfavour because of what they were alleged to have done to the place last time? That you didn't once again put aside your much vaunted "loyalty" to me and play on your "loyalty" to him instead? You didn't know of his intention to phone me and threaten to bring about my dismissal if I continued, as he put it, to "defy" the rules and regulations of the local authority? And this over a subject which came strictly under my jurisdiction and did not require consultation with him or his commitee at all?'

She answered steadily, 'I repeat that I knew nothing about it, but I can see that no matter how much I declare my innocence, you won't believe me.'

She caught the grin on Roseanna's face. Richard saw it too, and with an impatient movement dismissed his secretary.

When they were alone she said, endeavouring to keep her voice steady, 'I'm going to give in my notice. After this, I know I haven't a hope of ever gaining your trust.'

He did not hesitate. He found a blank piece of paper and handed her his pen. 'If you'll write it out, my secretary will type it, then you can sign it.'

She could not believe it—he was so eager to see the back of her that he could not risk her changing her mind! She felt dazed, drained of vitality. As she wrote, she remembered Pearl's words. 'If he says he'll get rid of you, then, believe me, he will.'

When she had finished, he took the letter into his secretary's room. He returned, closed the door on the clatter of the typewriter and crossed to the window. Carolyn whispered, 'Richard.' He moved abruptly in response, but did not turn. 'I had nothing to do with

175

this. Please believe me.'

He did not seem to hear, and continued to stare out of the window.

Roseanna came in. 'Here you are, Miss Lyle. All you've got to do is sign it.'

Her grin was malevolent and gloating, like a mouse that had just caught a cat. She left them alone again. Carolyn signed her name, folded the letter and handed it to Richard. He took it and said, 'I'll send you a formal acceptance.'

That was all. No regrets, no thanks, nothing. She returned to her duties. Only a short time now, she told herself, and she would never see Richard Hindon again.

She was half-way through her term of notice when she met Pearl and Graham on the steps of the Library. They were holding hands.

'We're going out for the evening,' Pearl said. 'We're having dinner somewhere.' She looked shyly at Graham. 'Shall we tell her?' He nodded. 'It's a celebration dinner, Carolyn. We're engaged.'

Carolyn was overjoyed and said so. 'Where's the ring? When's it to be?'

Pearl laughed. 'We're choosing the ring soon. And oh, it won't be for two or three months yet.'

Carolyn walked with them to the car park. 'I'm really delighted,' she told them.

They were standing by the side of Graham's car, when Richard appeared. Graham called to him, 'Are you going to congratulate us too, Richard? We're telling the world about our engagement.'

Richard took his outstretched hand and shook it hard. 'My dear chap, I'm really delighted.'

They laughed. 'Carolyn's just said that.'

Richard looked at her for the first time for days. 'At least we have something in common.'

Carolyn flushed, detecting the sarcasm, but Pearl

and Graham laughed again, too happy to care. They drove away, still laughing.

'Can I give you a lift, Miss Lyle?'

Carolyn heard the curt tone and held her head high. 'No, thank you.' She saw him shrug before she walked away.

She had had a tussle with her uncle when she had told him about her resignation. She hadn't told him why she had done it. She pretended that she did not feel right in that sort of work.

One morning Richard called her into his room. She wondered wearily what she had done this time and hardened herself in advance to his anger.

But he was not angry. There was compassion in his eyes as he told her to sit down.

'I'll stand,' she said.

'Sit down.' It was a command and she had to obey.

He sat too, and said gently, 'Your grandmother has just telephoned.'

Her heart began to thump painfully and she half rose from her seat. 'She's ill?'

'She's perfectly well.' Carolyn sat down. 'It's your father.'

She paled. 'My—my *father*?'

He nodded. 'He's apparently very ill. He's in hospital and is asking for you.'

'But I haven't seen my father for years. Not since I was five.'

'I know that.' He was still speaking gently. 'But it seems that he hasn't forgotten you and since he's asking to see you, I think you should go.' He told her the name of the hospital. 'It's nearly forty miles from here.'

'But—but how do I get there?'

He stood up. 'I'll take you.'

'But you can't do that. It's much too far. There's your work——'

'I said I'll take you. While you're getting your coat,

I'll have a word with Graham. He can take over for the day.'

He led her to the car, holding her elbow to steady her. Then they were on their way.

'It's a long journey,' she murmured, still in a daze. 'It'll take a long time.'

My father, she was thinking, he's sent for me. Seventeen years since I've seen him. What will he look like? My father sent for me. The words repeated themselves like a recorded message. Half-way there, they stopped for coffee. Then they hurried on.

At the hospital, Richard left her to greet her father alone. She knew she would not recognise him. She counted the beds and found the fifth one along on the left. The man in the bed was staring at her. He looked old and ill. He was frail and lifeless, but life seemed to flood back into him as he watched her approach. As she drew near, he stretched out his hand.

'My daughter,' he said, 'my daughter, grown up, a young lady.' She stood beside him. She made herself smile. She felt no sense of belonging to this man, this stranger, and she was dismayed by the numbness that had taken away her feelings.

'Hallo, Father,' she whispered, and the voice was not her own. She put her hand in his and sat on the chair beside the bed.

He couldn't take his eyes off her face. 'It's like your mother come back. When I saw you first I thought, "It's Beth come back." You're so like her, I can't believe it.' Carolyn could not take in what he was saying. 'Where's that lovely hair, dear? Had it cut off?'

'Yes, a little while ago. How did you know I had long hair?'

'Oh, your gran kept in touch. Sent me pictures of you. I've watched you grow up without you knowing it. I didn't want her to tell you, I thought it might upset you to hear about me.' His head sank back on to the pillows. 'I've drifted a bit. Got married again. It didn't work out. I missed your mother so. I couldn't have you with me. You were in the best place with your uncle taking care of you, with money and all that.'

Richard came, stood beside Carolyn and smiled down at the man in the bed. 'Hallo, Mr. Lyle.' He stretched out his hand and took the other man's in his.

'Come on, Carolyn, my dear. Who's this? Your young man? What's his name?' She told him. Her father's eyes lit up again. 'Richard? You her young man?'

He was growing excited. Richard glanced at Carolyn's bent head, then faced her father squarely. 'Yes, Mr. Lyle. I'm her young man.'

'Getting married, are you?' He didn't wait for an answer. 'You take care of her, Richard, won't you? You'll look after her better than I ever did?'

'Don't worry, Mr. Lyle, I'll take good care of her.' He bent low and whispered, 'She's worth taking care of.'

Her father laughed and patted Richard's hand, still in his. 'When's it to be? Soon, eh? Tell me in good time. I'll be there at your wedding. I'll be better by then.' He was flushed and, Carolyn felt, more excited than was good for him. 'Now I know this, my lad, I'll get so fit they'll be glad to get rid of me.' They talked for a while, then a nurse told them it was time to go.

Her father's arms went round her neck and she kissed him gently. 'Come and see me again, dear. I don't want to wait another seventeen years.' He shook Richard by the hand again. 'You wait until I tell all these other chaps. My daughter's getting married!'

Richard's arm round her waist held her close until they reached the door. Together they turned and waved and walked out of the hospital. He helped her into the car and they made for home.

Carolyn was silent. She was trying to rationalise her feelings, trying to explain away the numbness in her

179

mind. She felt as if she was under an anaesthetic, because when she thought about her father there was no reaction, nothing at all. After seventeen years she had seen him again and it hadn't meant a thing.

On the way they had a meal and then continued their journey. Some time later Richard glanced at her, frowned and pulled into a parking bay, saying he wanted a rest. Slowly Carolyn came back to life. The torpidity ebbed away and sensation returned, and with it came bitterness and pain. She began to talk at last.

'There was no need for you to tell all those lies, no need to tell him we were engaged. What will you do,' she challenged, 'when he gets better and comes out of there and asks about the wedding again? How will you get out of that one?'

She knew she was being unfair. He had after all only said it for her sake. He answered quietly, taking her hand,

'Carolyn, my dear, I had a word with the Sister. He won't come out of there. He isn't expected to live much longer. It's his heart, and he's in a bad way.'

She whispered, 'He's going to die?'

Richard nodded. So the man she had rejected as worthless for as long as she could remember, the father she had found again, was going out of her life once more, this time for good. 'Her own flesh and blood'—her uncle's words rang in her ears. Now she knew their true meaning. The dam burst, the waters flooded through.

'Richard, oh, Richard,' she sobbed, and groped towards him. Then she pulled away. She couldn't ask for comfort there. But his arms came out and he gathered her to him and as she cried, he stroked her hair and whispered words of comfort.

Her sobbing lessened and stopped and his arms slackened their hold. She sat upright, using the handkerchief he had pressed into her hand. 'I'm sorry,' she mumbled, and he smiled at her and started the engine.

The Downs were in sight now and beckoning them on. They were nearly home.

She said, dully, 'So you were quite safe in what you said to my father. You knew all the time you were making promises you would never have to keep.'

'Yes,' he agreed quietly, 'I was quite safe.'

He drew up outside her house. 'Thank you very much for taking me,' she said, and got out.

He joined her on the pavement. 'I'll come in and have a word with your grandmother.'

He followed her into the house. Carolyn introduced Richard and watched her grandmother's eyes open wide. She must have expected Richard to look very different from the good-looking, pleasant-mannered man in front of her. They went into the sitting-room and Richard told her what he had learned from the hospital Sister. He spoke gently and compassionately and Carolyn could almost feel her warming to him.

'Of course he's putting on the charm,' she told herself sourly. 'It's in his interests, isn't it, if he impresses the chairman's mother?' But she knew she was being unfair because, whatever he was, he was not an opportunist, rather the opposite, in fact.

He got up to leave and took Carolyn's hand. 'Don't come in tomorrow if you don't feel like it. I'll understand.'

She thanked him. 'But I'll probably be all right.' She looked purposefully into his eyes. 'After all, my days there are numbered. I want to make the most of the time I have left.'

He dropped her hand abruptly, took his leave of her grandmother and went away.

'Now there's a nice man,' Mrs. Bullman said, lifting up the net curtain and waving to him. 'Can't see why Austin doesn't like him.' She looked at her granddaughter's tear-stained face. 'Have a wash, dear, then you can tell me all about it.'

So Carolyn tidied herself and sat on her bed and stared at her reflection. What was it her father had said? 'I thought it was Beth walking in. You're so like her, I couldn't believe it.' Where was that photograph? She studied it, moved her eyes to the mirror, back to the picture and back yet again. Yes, of course there was a resemblance, a definite family likeness. Why hadn't she seen it before? The curve of the mouth, the soft curling hair, the expression in the eyes, the identical nose. Those features—now she could see how they matched her own. There was no doubt about it. She felt as though she had been given a gift which was beyond price.

She replaced the photograph with loving care and ran to the sitting room to tell her grandmother everything she wanted to know.

CHAPTER TEN

Two days later, Carolyn's father died. 'Don't you worry, dear,' her grandmother said. 'Your uncle will go to the funeral.'

It was quickly over and Austin came home with the items which her father had wished her to have.

'There was no money, my dear,' Austin said. 'And no property to dispose of. He'd rented a couple of rooms.' He looked at the things in his hands. 'These were your mother's. He wanted you to have them.' He gave her a watch, a couple of rings, a brooch and a necklace. In a box, wrapped in tissue, was a gold locket. Inside were miniatures of her mother and father taken when they were newly married. Tenderly she put it away.

Her last day at the library passed quickly. She had not seen much of Richard, but whenever they had passed each other he had smiled. He seemed to have no animosity towards her now, probably, she thought bitterly, because she would soon have gone from under his feet. He could afford to be pleasant.

She said goodbye to all the staff, and even Miss Blane seemed sorry to see her go. They shook her by the hand and Keith said he could quite understand her wanting to leave. 'It's the people you've had to work with—they're shocking!' He glowered round him and everyone laughed.

Graham, standing by his desk upstairs, took her hands in his. He seemed happier these days, and although affected by her leaving, he obviously saw it in perspective. 'Don't give up, Carolyn. Get into another library, somewhere out of the area, where connections and influence won't count. You know what I mean?'

They smiled at each other and he asked, 'Seen

Richard yet?'

'No, I—I suppose I must say goodbye to him.'

'Don't look so scared, my dear. Come with me. I'll see if he's there.'

He knocked on Richard's door and beckoned to her to follow. Roseanna was there, too. 'Richard, Carolyn's come to say goodbye. I almost had to hold her hand—I think she thought you might eat her!' He laughed and left them.

She took a breath to steady herself, held out her hand and said, 'Goodbye, Mr. Hindon. In spite of everything, I've enjoyed working here.'

'Goodbye, Miss Lyle.' That was all he said. They shook hands and there was no smile, no message in his eyes. She went to the door. 'Goodbye, Mrs. Harvey.' Roseanna smiled and bowed her head graciously.

The door closed and her footsteps echoed back at her all along the corridor. She was walking out of Richard Hindon's life. And he had let her go.

Pearl went home with her. She was almost pretty nowadays, happiness and contentment giving a becoming softness to her too-regular features.

They talked at the corner of the road. 'I wish you weren't leaving, Carolyn. I can't understand why you gave up so quickly. I think you would have done well. After all, you've got the necessary intelligence.'

Carolyn laughed ruefully. 'That's about all I have got!'

Pearl laughed and they waved to each other. 'See you some time,' Pearl called, and went on her way.

Carolyn was alone that evening. Her grandmother was visiting a friend. She roamed round the house, unsettled and unbearably miserable. She decided to go out. She could not stay in the house with all that restlessness pecking at the shell of her mind trying to get out. She put on her coat and made for the Downs.

The evening was dull and brooding, the clouds a

metallic grey, hanging low in threatening folds. The brittle grass flicked against her shoes and the hard white scalp of chalk, from which it sprang, showed through the stiff green blades. The sea was grey and clear and seemed near enough to touch. The horizon was sharp, promising rain before morning.

Her footsteps quickened and grew frenzied in her efforts to throw off her thoughts, but they fluttered round her like moths around a bright light and she could not shake them off. She gave up and went home.

The doorbell rang. She frowned. Who was it—a friend of her grandmother's? Her uncle, perhaps. She opened the door, still wearing her coat. She gasped.

'Carolyn?' Richard smiled. 'May I come in?' He saw how she was dressed. 'Oh, I'm sorry. It didn't occur to me that you might have a date. But I won't keep you long.'

'I haven't—I mean, I've just come back. From a walk.'

'Alone?'

She nodded. 'Come in.'

They went into the sitting-room and she threw her coat over a chair. There was a throbbing in her temples and the palms of her hands were moist. They looked at each other.

'What did you want to see me about?' Her voice was thin and dry.

He looked round for an armchair and lowered himself into it as though his legs felt too tired to hold him upright. She sat opposite him. He leaned back and crossed his legs, seeming uneasy.

'I wondered if you had another job lined up.'

Her smile came and went. 'Not a thing. I'll have to go to an agency. I can't stay unemployed. We need the money I bring in.'

'Oh,' he said it shortly as though it clashed with a thought in his mind. 'I was going to suggest—if you'd liked the idea—that you might go to a library school for a year. There are a number in different parts of the

185

country. You take exams at the end of the course, and when you're qualified you could get quite a good position on the staff of any library.'

She frowned. Was this all he had come to tell her? But what had she expected—a plea for her to return? A 'we need you here' appeal from the heart? 'I didn't regard myself as good enough to think in those terms. I don't seem to have done very well while I was working at your library.'

He answered with another question. 'Haven't you thought about your future at all?'

She shrugged.

'Doesn't Shane come into it?'

'Shane?' She laughed without humour. 'Good heavens, no. He's out tonight with a girl. I never know which one.'

'And it doesn't worry you?'

'Why should it? There's nothing between us, except friendship.'

He sat forward. There seemed to be more life in him now.

'So you would be free to go to a library school if the finances were there to tide you over?'

She shrugged. 'Perhaps.' Her eyes were heavy. 'But I can't ask my uncle for money again for my education. I've got to support myself at least, if not my grandmother, from now on.'

'The local authority might give you a grant to go to library school.'

'You mean,' she commented bitterly, ' "Uncle's influence" again?'

'Not at all. They often help people in your position. In fact, I've made enquiries and one or two councillors have said it's almost a certainty you would get financial assistance if you asked for it.'

She could not throw off her bitterness. 'With strings attached, no doubt. Provided I returned to this area after I qualified and took up my job again in this library? Your library?'

He nodded.

'Then what would be the use?' she asked wearily. 'You wouldn't have me back.'

'Wouldn't I?'

She stood up. 'No, of course you wouldn't.' He stood too. 'You'd only reject me again.' Tears started to her eyes and she walked blindly to the door. 'You reject everyone who——' She stopped, aghast, and opened the door. 'I'll make some coffee.'

He was there in front of her, shutting the door and staring into her eyes. 'I've heard that somewhere before,' he said slowly. 'Finish that sentence.'

She tugged at the door, trying to open it. 'I'm going to make——'

He wrenched it out of her hand and shut it again. He caught at her roughly. 'Now will you finish that sentence? I reject everyone who——?' He waited, watching her through the long silence.

'Loves you,' she managed at last.

He held her at arms' length and said, taking his time, 'Do I take that to mean you love me?' His voice sounded odd.

She tried desperately to read his eyes. Should she tell him the truth? She couldn't help herself, it just came out. 'Yes.'

'Right.' He rolled the word round his tongue. 'Now watch me reject you!'

She was jerked against him and his kiss drew the breath from her body. She clung to him and he lifted her and carried her to the couch. He told her he loved her, had loved her for months, in fact he couldn't remember when he hadn't loved her.

'They say you never hear the one that hits you, and, my God, I didn't hear you. I was in love with you before I even knew I'd begun.'

'But, Richard, I thought you hated me.'

'At first, my darling, I simply didn't want to know. I

told you, I was a solitary,' he whispered against her ear, 'notice the past tense—then you came along and that was the end of my peace. You were a magnet. Wherever you were I wanted to be. Couldn't you see it? You tormented me by day and haunted my dreams at night. My God, the dreams I had about you!'

Then he murmured, his voice rough, 'That beautiful hair, Carolyn. When you had it cut, you almost broke my heart. Why did you do it?'

She turned her face to his jacket. 'To hurt you,' she said, 'as you were hurting me. But there were other reasons. I'll tell you one day.'

'And now I'll tell you a secret. With Graham's help —by then he had guessed my feelings for you—I found out the name of your hairdresser. I went to them and told them you were my fiancée and I was upset that you'd had your hair cut off and for sentimental reasons, I wanted to buy it back. They argued a bit, but in the end sold me one of the plaits. It's now in a drawer in my room.'

'You did that?' For a few moments, she was too moved to speak. 'So those promises you made to my father—you really meant them?'

'Every word, my darling. Did you really think I would lie to a man as ill as your father was?'

They were silent for a while. 'Did you know,' he said at last, 'that Hilary's husband is coming home soon?'

'So you'll be moving out of their house?'

'Yes, and in a few weeks I'll be moving into a new home—with you. How many children are we going to have? Three, isn't it?'

'So you remembered,' she whispered.

'I couldn't get it out of my mind,' he whispered back.

'I haven't said I'll marry you yet!'

'My sweet, it's a foregone conclusion. Otherwise, I'll....'

After that, there was no need for speech. His mouth

188

took hers. There was no gentleness about his lovemaking. She had not expected that there would be. That he was capable of it she knew by past experience, but to a man with his latent anger, his ruthlessness and his uncompromising attitude to all things, tenderness would not come easily. Such a man would demand total submission. He did, and he got it.

He whispered, searching her eyes, 'My darling, you didn't expect me to be gentle? If I loved you less, perhaps I could be, but....'

Her passionate response gave him his answer.

Some time later, a key was turned in the front door.

'Who's that?' Richard asked, reluctantly putting her from him. 'Your grandmother?'

She whispered, suddenly afraid, 'Darling, it could be my uncle.'

It was. Austin Bullman stood in the doorway, filling it with his bulk. He stared, frowned and stared again.

'What's this?' he asked briskly. 'What's all this about? What's going on?'

Richard stood and drew Carolyn up beside him. With a gesture of defiance she pushed her arm through his and glared at her uncle, daring him to disapprove.

'What's this?' Austin repeated, looking at Richard. 'Making love to my niece? Making a fool of me good and proper now?'

'Uncle,' Carolyn said, flushing and still defiant, 'we love each other. We're getting married.'

'So I see, my lady. I'd have to be blind not to. By God, he's done it again! He's played the trump card all right now, hasn't he? So you think it's checkmate, do you? Game, set *and* match to you, eh, Mr. Librarian?' Austin demanded, getting his metaphors and his pastimes somewhat mixed. 'What do you expect me to do—throw you out of the house? By God, I couldn't do that even if I wanted to.' He glanced at his niece. 'By the look of her, she'd go with you—she'd follow you to the ends of the earth.'

He confronted Richard, hands on hips, and glared at him. Then he reached out and took his hand in a hearty, pumping handshake. 'She's yours, Mr. Librarian Hindon. She's yours with my love. But look after her well, lad. Take good care of her. She's my own flesh and blood.'

Carolyn, with an uncharacteristically abandoned gesture, flung her arms round his neck and hugged him. 'Uncle, you're wonderful!'

Carefully he disengaged himself from her arms and straightened his collar. 'I know, lass, but there's no need to rub it in. And you can tell your Richard something else. I've got news for him—I've got him his new library.'

Now it was Richard's turn to shake hands, his face alight with pleasure. 'My word, this is a day,' he said. 'How did you do it, Alderman Bullman?'

'How? I wouldn't take "no" for an answer. You ought to know me, lad, by now.' He slapped Richard on the back and shouted with laughter. 'After all, look what my obstinacy at her interview,' his thumb moved towards his niece, 'got you—a fine-looking—and loving —young lass for a wife.' He whispered in Richard's ear, 'And don't wait too long. It doesn't do at all.'

In answer, Richard pulled Carolyn even closer.

'But, Uncle, what made you change your mind? You were always so against everything Richard wanted. Was it because you guessed about us?'

'My lass, I didn't know about you until I set foot in this house tonight. No, I'll tell you why.' He eased himself into a chair, motioning to the other two to do the same, crossed his arms and his legs and held the unwavering attention of his audience.

'I did it, lass, because I knew that in Richard Hindon I'd met my match. I gave in—not him. All the time, all through our battles and our arguments, he gave as good as he got. He's stuck to his principles through thick and thin. I tried to stop him in every way

I knew—even abused him to his face. But he woul[d] give an inch, and by God, that's what I like to see[. If] there's one thing I admire in a man it's that, what[ever] his views. I could see in the end he'd never be an E[stab]lishment man.' He swung his eyes to Richard. 'Yo[u're] just what us lot need, lad, good, strong, intelli[gent,] unyielding opposition.' He stood up. 'And you k[now] the way to my heart in the end, lad—by marrying [my] niece!'

He went to the door and turned. He saw that [they] hadn't even waited for him to go. They were in [each] other's arms.

'That's what I like to see,' he remarked to him[self.] 'By God, that's what I like to see!'

He closed the door behind him.

took hers. There was no gentleness about his lovemaking. She had not expected that there would be. That he was capable of it she knew by past experience, but to a man with his latent anger, his ruthlessness and his uncompromising attitude to all things, tenderness would not come easily. Such a man would demand total submission. He did, and he got it.

He whispered, searching her eyes, 'My darling, you didn't expect me to be gentle? If I loved you less, perhaps I could be, but. . . .'

Her passionate response gave him his answer.

Some time later, a key was turned in the front door.

'Who's that?' Richard asked, reluctantly putting her from him. 'Your grandmother?'

She whispered, suddenly afraid, 'Darling, it could be my uncle.'

It was. Austin Bullman stood in the doorway, filling it with his bulk. He stared, frowned and stared again.

'What's this?' he asked briskly. 'What's all this about? What's going on?'

Richard stood and drew Carolyn up beside him. With a gesture of defiance she pushed her arm through his and glared at her uncle, daring him to disapprove.

'What's this?' Austin repeated, looking at Richard. 'Making love to my niece? Making a fool of me good and proper now?'

'Uncle,' Carolyn said, flushing and still defiant, 'we love each other. We're getting married.'

'So I see, my lady. I'd have to be blind not to. By God, he's done it again! He's played the trump card all right now, hasn't he? So you think it's checkmate, do you? Game, set *and* match to you, eh, Mr. Librarian?' Austin demanded, getting his metaphors and his pastimes somewhat mixed. 'What do you expect me to do—throw you out of the house? By God, I couldn't do that even if I wanted to.' He glanced at his niece. 'By the look of her, she'd go with you—she'd follow you to the ends of the earth.'

He confronted Richard, hands on hips, and glared at him. Then he reached out and took his hand in a hearty, pumping handshake. 'She's yours, Mr. Librarian Hindon. She's yours with my love. But look after her well, lad. Take good care of her. She's my own flesh and blood.'

Carolyn, with an uncharacteristically abandoned gesture, flung her arms round his neck and hugged him. 'Uncle, you're wonderful!'

Carefully he disengaged himself from her arms and straightened his collar. 'I know, lass, but there's no need to rub it in. And you can tell your Richard something else. I've got news for him—I've got him his new library.'

Now it was Richard's turn to shake hands, his face alight with pleasure. 'My word, this is a day,' he said. 'How did you do it, Alderman Bullman?'

'How? I wouldn't take "no" for an answer. You ought to know me, lad, by now.' He slapped Richard on the back and shouted with laughter. 'After all, look what my obstinacy at her interview,' his thumb moved towards his niece, 'got you—a fine-looking—and loving —young lass for a wife.' He whispered in Richard's ear, 'And don't wait too long. It doesn't do at all.'

In answer, Richard pulled Carolyn even closer.

'But, Uncle, what made you change your mind? You were always so against everything Richard wanted. Was it because you guessed about us?'

'My lass, I didn't know about you until I set foot in this house tonight. No, I'll tell you why.' He eased himself into a chair, motioning to the other two to do the same, crossed his arms and his legs and held the unwavering attention of his audience.

'I did it, lass, because I knew that in Richard Hindon I'd met my match. *I* gave in—not him. All the time, all through our battles and our arguments, he gave as good as he got. He's stuck to his principles through thick and thin. I tried to stop him in every way

I knew—even abused him to his face. But he wouldn't give an inch, and by God, that's what I like to see! If there's one thing I admire in a man it's that, whatever his views. I could see in the end he'd never be an Establishment man.' He swung his eyes to Richard. 'You're just what us lot need, lad, good, strong, intelligent, unyielding opposition.' He stood up. 'And you knew the way to my heart in the end, lad—by marrying my niece!'

He went to the door and turned. He saw that they hadn't even waited for him to go. They were in each other's arms.

'That's what I like to see,' he remarked to himself. 'By God, that's what I like to see!'

He closed the door behind him.

Why the smile?

... because she has just received her **Free Harlequin Romance Catalogue!**

... and now she has a complete listing of the many, many Harlequin Romances still available.

... and now she can pick out titles by her favorite authors or fill in missing numbers for her library.

You too may have a **Free Harlequin Romance Catalogue** (and a smile!), simply by mailing in the coupon below.